A WORD ABOUT
THE LOVERS . . .

One of the milestones of modern science
fiction, The Lovers virtually turned the field
upside down with its portrayal of a sexual
liaison between a human and an alien. Originally published in a much shorter version in
a science-fiction magazine in the early 50's,
the novel now appears in a definitive edition,
newly revised by the author.

This landmark work, whose emotional ap-
peal and narrative compulsion remain reward-
ingly fresh, makes a dramatic and memorable
statement about the essentials of life and
death and love.

". . . a book which is part fantasy, part
science fiction and chock full of eroticism
. . . the novel is enjoyable because of the
conviction and energy of the author."
— *The New York Daily News*

THE

❧ Lovers ❧

Philip José Farmer

A Del Rey Book

BALLANTINE BOOKS • NEW YORK

A Del Rey Book
Published by Ballantine Books

Library of Congress Catalog Card Number: 78-19723

ISBN 0-345-28691-X

Manufactured in the United States of America

First Edition: May 1979

Paperback format
First Edition: March 1980

Cover painting by Les Katz
Special lettering and design by David Myers

To Sam Mines,
who saw deeper than the others

"**I**'VE got to get out," Hal Yarrow could hear someone muttering from a great distance. "There must be a way out."

He woke up with a start, and he realized that he had been the one talking. Moreover, what he had said as he emerged from his dream had no connection at all to it. His half-waking words and the dream were two discrete events.

But what had he meant by those mumbled words? And where was he? Had he actually traveled in time or had he experienced a subjective dream? It had been so vivid that he was slow in returning to this level of the world.

A look at the man sitting beside him cleared his mind. He was in the coach to Sigmen City in the year 550 B.S. (Old Style 3050 A.D., his scholar's mind told him.) He was not, as in the time travel? dream? on a strange planet many light-years from here, many years from now. Nor was he face to face with the glorious Isaac Sigmen, the Forerunner, real be his name.

The man beside him looked sidewise at Hal. He was a lean fellow with high cheekbones, straight black hair, and brown eyes which had a slight Mongoloid fold. He was dressed in the light blue uniform of the engineering class and wore on his left breast an aluminum emblem which indicated he was in the upper echelon. Probably, he was an electronics engineer with a degree from one of the better trade schools.

The man cleared his throat, and he said, in American, "A thousand pardons, *abba*. I know I shouldn't be talking to you without permission. But you did say something to me as you awoke. And, since you're in this cabin, you have temporarily equated yourself. In any event, I've been dying to ask you a question. I'm not called Nosy Sam for nothing."

He laughed nervously and said, "Couldn't help overhearing what you told the stewardess when she challenged your right to sit here. Did I hear you right, or did you actually tell her you was a *goat?*"

Hal smiled and said, "No. Not a goat. I'm a *joat*. From the initial letters of *jack-of-all-trades*. You weren't too mistaken, however. In the professional fields, a *joat* has about as much prestige as a goat."

He sighed and thought of the humiliations endured because he had chosen not to be a narrow specialist. He looked out the window because he did not want to encourage his seatmate to talk. He saw a bright glow far off and up, undoubtedly a military spaceship entering the atmosphere. The few civilian ships made a slower and unobtrusive descent.

From the height of sixty thousand meters, he looked down on the curve of the North American continent. It was a blaze of light with, here and there, some small bands of darkness and an occasional large band. The latter would be a mountain range or body of water on which man had not yet succeeded in building residences or industries. The great city. Megalopolis. Think—only three hundred years ago, the entire continent had a mere two million population. In another fifty years—unless something catastrophic happened, such as war between the Haijac Union and the Israeli Republics—the population of North America would be fourteen, maybe fifteen, billion!

The only area in which living room was deliberately denied was the Hudson Bay Wildlife Preserve. He had left the Preserve only fifteen minutes ago, yet he felt sick because he would not be able to return to it for a long time.

He sighed again. The Hudson Bay Wildlife Preserve. Trees by the thousands, mountains, broad blue lakes, birds, foxes, rabbits, even, the rangers said, bobcats. There were so few, however, that in ten years they would be added to the long list of extinct animals.

Hal could breathe in the Preserve, could feel unconstricted. Free. He also could feel lonely and uneasy at times. But he was just beginning to get over that when his research among the twenty French-speaking inhabitants of the Preserve was finished.

The man beside him shifted as if he were trying to get up courage to speak again to the professional beside him. After some nervous coughs, he said, "Sigmen help me, I hope I ain't offended you. But I was wondering . . . "

Hal Yarrow felt offended because the man was presuming too much. Then, he reminded himself of what the Forerunner had said. *All men are brothers, though some are more favored by the father than others.* And it was not this man's fault that the first-class cabin had been filled with people with higher priorities and Hal had been forced to choose between taking a later coach or sitting with the lower echelon.

"It's *shib* with me," said Yarrow. He explained.

The man said, "Ah!" as if he were relieved. "Then, you won't perhaps mind one more question? Don't call me Nosy Sam for nothing, like I said. Ha! Ha!"

"No, I don't mind," said Hal Yarrow. "A *joat*, though a jack-of-all-trades, does not make all sciences his field. He *is* confined to one particular discipline, but he tries to understand as much of all the specialized branches of it as he can. For instance, I am a linguistic *joat*. Instead of restricting myself to one of the many areas of linguistics, I have a good general knowledge of that science. This ability enables me to correlate what is going on in all its fields, to search out things in one specialty which might be of interest to a man in another specialty, and to notify him of this item. Otherwise, the specialist, who doesn't have the time to read the hundreds of journals in his field alone, might be missing something that would aid him.

"All the professional studies have their own *joats* doing this. Actually, I'm very lucky to be in this branch of science. If I were, for example, a medical *joat,* I'd be overwhelmed. I'd have to work with a team of *joats*. Even then, I couldn't be a genuine jack-of-all-trades. I'd have to restrict myself to one area of medical science. So tremendous is the number of publications in each specialty of medicine—or of electronics or physics or just about any science you might want to mention—that no man or team could correlate the entire discipline. Fortunately, my interest has always been in linguistics. I am, in a way, favored. I even have time to do a little research myself and so add to the avalanche of papers.

"I use computers, of course, but even the most complex computer complex is an idiot savant. It takes a human mind—a rather keen one, if I do say so myself—to perceive that certain items have more significance than others and to make a meaningful association between or among them. Then I point these out to the specialists, and they study them. A *joat,* you might say, is a creative correlator.

"However," he added, "that is at the cost of my personal time for sleeping. I must work twelve hours a day or more for the glory and benefit of the Sturch."

His last comment was to ensure that the fellow, if he happened to be an Uzzite or a stool for the Uzzites, could not report that he was cheating the Sturch. Hal did not think it likely that the man was anything other than what he looked, but he did not care to take the chance.

A red light flashed on the wall above the cabin entrance, and a recording told the passengers to fasten their belts. Ten seconds later, the coach began decelerating; a minute later, the vehicle dipped sharply and began dropping at the rate—so Hal had been told—of a thousand meters a minute. Now that they were closer to the ground, Hal could see that Sigmen City (called Montreal until ten years ago when the capital of the Haijac Union had been moved from Rek, Iceland, to this site) was not a single blaze of light. Dark spots, probably parks, could be made out here and there, and the thin black ribbon winding by it was the Prophet (once St. Lawrence) River. The *palis* of Sigmen City rose five hundred meters in the air; each one housed at least a hundred thousand selves, and there were three hundred of this size in the area of the city proper.

In the middle of the metropolis was a square occupied by trees and government buildings, none of which was over fifty stories high. This was the University of Sigmen City, where Hal Yarrow did his work.

Hal, however, lived in the *pali* nearby, and it was toward this that he rode the belt after getting off the coach. Now, he felt strongly something that he had not noticed—consciously—all the days of his waking life. Not until after he had made this research trip to the Hudson Bay Preserve. And that was the crowd, the densely packed, jostling, pushing, and odorous mass of humanity.

They pressed in on him without knowing that he was there except as another body, another man, faceless, only a brief obstacle to their destination.

"Great Sigmen!" he muttered. "I must have been deaf, dumb, and blind! Not to have known! I *hate* them!"

He felt himself turn hot with guilt and shame. He looked into the faces of those around him as if they could see his hate, his guilt, his contrition, on his face. But they did not; they could not. To them, he was only another man, one to be treated with some respect if they encountered him personally because he was a professional. But not here, not on the belt carrying this flood of flesh down the thoroughfare. He was just another pack of blood and bones cemented by tissue and bound in skin. One of them and, therefore, nothing.

Shaken by this sudden revelation, Hal stepped off the belt. He wanted to get away from them, for he felt that he owed them an apology. And, at the same time, he felt like striking them.

A few steps from the belt, and above him, was the plastic lip of Pali No. 30, University Fellowship Residence. Inside this mouth, he felt no better, though he had lost the feeling he should apologize to those on the belt. There was no reason why they should know how he had suddenly been revolted. They had not seen the betraying flush on his face.

And even that was nonsense, he told himself, though he bit his lip as he did so. Those on the belt could not possibly have guessed. Not, that is, unless they, too, felt the same pressing-in and disgust. And, if they did, who were they to point him out?

He was among his own now, men and women clothed in the plastic baggy uniforms of the professional with the plaid design and the winged foot on the left chest. The only difference between male and female was that the women wore floor-length skirts over their trousers, nets over their hair, and some wore the veil. The latter was an article not too uncommon but dying out now, a custom retained by the older women or the more conservative of the young. Once honored, it now marked a woman as old-fashioned. This, despite the fact that the truecaster occasionally praised the veil and lamented its passing.

Hal spoke to several he passed but did not stop to talk. He saw Doctor Olvegssen, his department head, from a distance. He paused to see if Olvegssen wished to speak to him. Even this he did because the doctor was the only man with the authority to make him regret not paying his respects.

But Olvegssen evidently was busy, for he waved at Hal, called out, "Aloha," and walked on. Olvegssen was an old man; he used greetings and phrases popular in his youth.

Yarrow breathed with relief. Though he had thought he was eager to discuss his stay among the French-speaking natives of the Preserve, he now found that he did not want to talk to anybody. Not now. Maybe tomorrow. But not now.

Hal Yarrow waited by the door of the lift while the keeper checked the prospective passengers to determine who had priority. When the doors of the lift shaft opened, the keeper gave Hal's key back to him. He said, "You're first, *abba*."

"Sigmen bless," said Hal. He stepped into the lift and stood against the wall near the door while the others were identified and ranked.

The waiting was not long, for the keeper had been on his job for years and knew almost everybody by sight. Nevertheless, he had to go through the formality. Every once in a while, one of the residents was promoted or demoted. If the keeper had made the mistake of not recognizing the new shift in status, he would have been reported. His years at this post indicated that he knew his job well.

Forty people jammed into the lift, the keeper shook his castanets, and the door closed. The lift shot up swiftly enough to make everybody's knees bend; it continued to accelerate, for this was an express. At the thirtieth floor, the lift stopped automatically, and the doors opened. Nobody stepped out; perceiving this, the optical mechanism of the lift shut the doors, and the lift continued upward.

Three more stops with nobody stepping out. Then, half the crowd left. Hal drew in a deep breath, for if it had seemed crowded on the streets and on the ground floor, it was crushing inside the lift. Ten more stories, a journey in the same silence as that which had preceded it, every man and woman seeming intent on the truecaster's voice coming from the speaker in the ceiling. Then, the doors opened at Hal's floor.

The hallways were fifteen feet wide, room enough at this time of day. Nobody was in sight, and Hal was glad. If he had refused to chat for a few minutes with his neighbors, he would have been regarded as strange. That might have meant talk, and talk meant trouble, an explanation to his floor *gapt* at least. A heart-to-heart talk, a lecture, and Forerunner only knew what else.

He walked a hundred meters. Then, seeing the door to his *puka,* he stopped.

His heart had suddenly begun hammering, and his hands shook. He wanted to turn around and go back down the lift.

That, he told himself, was unreal behavior. He should not be feeling this way.

Besides, Mary would not be home for fifteen minutes at least.

He pushed open the door (no locks on the professional level, of course) and walked in. The walls began glowing and in ten seconds were at full bright. At the same time, the *tridi* sprang into life size on the wall opposite him, and the voices of the actors blared out. He jumped. Saying, "Great Sigmen!" under his breath, he hastened forward and turned off the wall. He knew that Mary had left it on, ready to spring into life when he walked in. He also knew that he had told her so many times how it surprised him that she could not possibly have forgotten. Which meant that she was doing it on purpose, consciously or unconsciously.

He shrugged and told himself that from now on he would not mention the matter. If she thought that he was no longer bothered by it, she might forget to leave it on.

Then, again, she might guess why he had suddenly become silent about her supposed forgetfulness. She might continue with the hope that he would eventually be unnerved, lose his temper, and start shouting at her. And, once more, she would have won a round, for she would refuse to argue back, would infuriate him by her silence and martyred look, and make him even angrier.

Then, of course, she would have to carry out her duty, however painful to her. She would, at the end of the month, go to the block *gapt* and report. And that would mean one more of many black crosses on his Morality Rating, which he would have to erase by some strenuous effort. And these efforts, if he made them—and he was getting tired of making them— would mean time lost from some more—dare he say it even to himself?—worthwhile project.

And if he protested to her that she was keeping him from advancing in his profession, from making more money, from moving into a larger *puka,* then he would have to listen to her sad, reproachful voice asking him if he actually wanted her to commit an *unreal* act. Would he ask her not to tell the truth, to lie by either omission or commission? He surely could not do that, for then both her self and his self would be in grave danger. Never would they see the glorious face of the Forerunner, and never . . . and so on and on—he helpless to answer back.

Yet, she was always asking him why he did not love her. And, when he replied that he did, she continued to say he did not. Then it was his turn to ask her if she thought he was lying. He was not; and if she called him a liar, then he would have to report her to the block *gapt.* Now, sheerly illogical, she would weep and say that she knew he did not love her. If he really did, he could not dream of telling the *gapt* about her.

When he protested that she thought it was *shib* for her to report him, he was answered with more tears. Or would be if he continued to fall into her trap. But he swore again and told himself that he would not.

Hal Yarrow walked through the living room, five-by-three meters, into the only other room—except the unmentionable—the kitchen. In the three- by two-and-a-half-meter room, he swung the stove down from the wall near the ceiling, dialed the proper code on its instrument panel, and walked back into the living room. Here he took off his jacket, crushed it into a ball, and stuffed it under a chair. He knew that Mary might find it and scold him for it, but he did not care.

He was, at the moment, too tired to reach up to the ceiling and pull down a hook.

A low pinging sound came from the kitchen. Supper was ready.

Hal decided to leave the correspondence until after he had eaten. He went into the unmentionable to wash his face and hands. Automatically, he murmured the ablution prayer, "May I wash off unreality as easily as water removes this dirt, so Sigmen wills it."

After cleaning himself, he pressed the button by the portrait of Sigmen above the washbasin. For a second, the face of the Forerunner stared at him, the long, lean face with a shock of bright red hair, big projecting ears, straw-colored and very thick eyebrows that met above the huge hooked nose with flaring nostrils, the pale blue eyes, the long orange-red beard, the lips thin as a knife's edge. Then, the face began to dim, to fade out. Another second, and the Forerunner was gone, replaced by a mirror.

Hal was allowed to look into this mirror just long enough to assure himself his face was clean and to comb his hair. There was nothing to keep him from standing before it past the allotted time, but he had never transgressed on himself. Whatever his faults, vanity was not one of them. Or so he had always told himself.

Yet, he lingered perhaps a little too long. And he saw the broad shoulders of a tall man, the face of a man thirty years old. His hair, like the Forerunner's, was red, but darker, almost bronze. His forehead was high and broad, his eyebrows were a dark brown, his widely-spaced eyes were a dark gray, his nose was straight and of normal size, his upper lip was a trifle too long, his lips were full, his chin a shade too prominent.

Hal pressed the button again. The silver of the mirror darkened, broke into streaks of brightness. Then it darkened again and firmed into the portrait of Sigmen. For the flicker of an eyelid, Hal saw his image superimposed on Sigmen's; then, his features faded, were absorbed by the Forerunner, the mirror was gone, and the portrait was there.

Hal left the unmentionable and went to the kitchen. He made sure the door was locked (the kitchen door and unmentionable door were the only ones capable of being locked), for he did not want to be surprised by Mary while eating. He opened the stove door, removed the warm box, placed the box on a table swung down from the wall, and pushed the stove back up to the ceiling. Then, he opened the box and ate his meal. After dropping the plastic container down the recovery-chute opening in the wall, he went back to the unmentionable and washed his hands.

While he was doing so, he heard Mary call his name.

2

HAL hesitated for a moment before answering, though he did not know why or even think of it. Then, he said, "In here, Mary."

Mary said, "Oh! Of course, I knew you'd be there, if you were home. Where else could you be?"

Unsmiling, he walked into the living room. "Must you be so sarcastic, even after I've been gone so long?"

Mary was a tall woman, only half a head shorter than Hal. Her hair was pale blond and drawn tightly back from her forehead to a heavy coil at the nape of her neck. Her eyes were light blue. Her features were regular and petite but were marred by very thin lips. The baggy high-necked shirt and loose floor-length skirt she wore prevented any observer from knowing what kind of figure she had. Hal himself did not know.

Mary said, "I wasn't being sarcastic, Hal. Just realistic. Where else could you be? All you had to do was say, 'Yes.' And you *would* have to be in there"—she pointed at the door to the unmentionable—"when I come home. You seem to spend all your time in there or at your studies. Almost as if you were trying to hide from me."

"A fine homecoming," he said.

"You haven't kissed me," she said.

"Ah, yes," he replied. "That's my duty. I forgot."

"It shouldn't be a duty," she said. "It should be a joy."

"It's hard to enjoy kissing lips that snarl," he said.

To his surprise, Mary, instead of replying angrily, began to weep. At once, he felt ashamed.

"I'm sorry," he said. "But you'll have to admit you weren't in a very good mood when you came in."

He went to her and tried to put his arms around her, but she turned away from him. Nevertheless, he kissed her on the side of her mouth as she turned her head.

"I don't want you to do that because you feel sorry for me or because it's your duty," she said. "I want you to do it because you love me."

"But I do love you," he said for what seemed like the thousandth time since they had married. Even to himself, he sounded unconvincing. Yet—he told himself—he did love her. He had to.

"You have a very nice way of showing it," she said.

"Let's forget what happened and start all over again," he said. "Here."

And he started to kiss her, but she backed away.

"What in H is the matter with you?" he said.

"You have given me my greeting kiss," she said. "You must not start getting sensual. This is not the time or place."

He threw his hands up in the air.

"Who's getting sensual? I wanted to act as if you had just come in the door. Is it worse to have one more kiss than prescribed than it is to quarrel? The trouble with you, Mary, is that you're absolutely literal-minded. Don't you know that the Forerunner himself didn't demand that his prescriptions be taken literally? He himself said that circumstances sometimes warranted modifications!"

"Yes, and he also said that we must beware of rationalizing ourselves into departing from his law. We must first confer with a *gapt* about the reality of our behavior."

"Oh, of course!" he said. "I'll phone our good guardian angel *pro tempore* and ask him if it's all right if I kiss you again!"

"That's the only safe thing to do," she said.

"Great Sigmen!" he shouted. "I don't know whether to laugh or cry! But I do know that I don't understand you! I never will!"

"Say a prayer to Sigmen," she said. "Ask him to give you reality. Then, we will have no difficulty."

"Say a prayer yourself," he said. "It takes two to make a quarrel. You're just as responsible as I am."

"I'll talk to you later when you're not so angry," she said. "I have to wash and eat."

"Never mind me," he replied. "I'll be busy until bedtime. I have to catch up on my Sturch business before I report to Olvegssen."

"And I'll bet you're happy you have to," she said. "I was looking forward to a nice talk. After all, you haven't said a word of your trip to the Preserve."

He did not reply.

She said, "You needn't bite your lip at me!"

He took a portrait of Sigmen down from the wall and unfolded it on a chair. Then he swung down his projector-magnifier from the wall, inserted the letter in it, and set the controls. After putting on his unscrambling goggles and sticking the phone in his ear, he sat down in the chair. He grinned as he did so. Mary must have seen the grin, and she probably wondered what caused it, but she did not ask. If she had, she would not have been answered. He could not tell her that he got a certain amusement from sitting on the Forerunner's portrait. She would have been shocked or would have pretended to be, he was never sure about her reactions. In any event, she had no sense of humor worth considering, and he did not intend to tell her anything that would downrate his M.R.

Hal pressed the button that activated the projector and then sat back, though not relaxedly. Immediately, the magnification of the film sprang up on the wall opposite him. Mary, not having goggles on, could see nothing except a blank wall. At the same time, he heard the voice recorded on the film.

First, as always with an official letter, the face of

the Forerunner appeared on the wall. The voice said, "Praise to Isaac Sigmen, in whom reality resides and from whom all truth flows! May he bless us, his followers, and confound his enemies, the disciples of the *unshib* Backrunner!"

There was a pause in the voice and a break in the projection for the viewer to send forth a prayer of his own. Then, a single word—*woggle*—flashed on the wall, and the speaker continued. "Devout believer Hal Yarrow:

"Here is the first of a list of words that have appeared recently in the vocabulary of the American-speaking population of the Union. This word—*woggle* —originated in the Department of Polynesia and spread radially to all the American-speaking peoples of the departments of North America, Australia, Japan, and China. Strangely, it has not yet made an appearance in the Department of South America, which, as you doubtless know, is contiguous to North America."

Hal Yarrow smiled, though there was a time when statements of this type had enraged him. When would the senders of these letters ever realize that he was not only a highly educated man but a broadly educated one, too? In this particular case, even the semiliterates of the lower classes should know where South America was, for the reason that the Forerunner had many times mentioned that continent in his *The Western Talmud* and *The Real World and Time*. It was true, however, that the schoolteachers of the unpros might never have thought to point out the location of South America to their pupils, even if they themselves knew.

"*Woggle*," continued the speaker, "was first reported on the island of Tahiti. This island lies in the center of the Polynesian Department and is inhabited by people descended from Australians who colonized it after the Apocalyptic War. Tahiti is, at present, used as a military spaceship base.

"*Woggle* apparently spread from there, but its use has been confined mainly to unprofessionals. The exception is the professional space personnel. We feel there is some connection between the appearance of the word and the fact that spacefarers were the first to use it—as far as we know.

"Truecasters have asked permission to use this word on the air, but this has been denied until further study.

"The word itself, as far as can be determined at this date, is used as adjective, noun, and verb. It contains a basically derogatory meaning close to, but not equivalent to, the linguistically acceptable words *fouled-up* and *jinxed*. In addition, it contains the meaning of something strange, otherworldly; in a word, unrealistic.

"You are hereby ordered to investigate the word *woggle,* following Plan No. ST–LIN–476 unless you have received an order with a higher priority number. In either case, you will reply to this letter not later than 12th Fertility, 550 B.S."

Hal ran the letter to the end. Fortunately, the other three words had lower priority. He did not have to accomplish the impossible: investigate all four at once.

But he would have to leave in the morning after reporting to Olvegssen. Which meant not even bothering to unpack his stuff, living for days in the clothes he was wearing, perhaps not having time to have them cleaned.

Not that he did not wish to get away. It was just that he was tired and wished to rest before going on this trip.

What rest? he asked himself after removing the goggles and looking at Mary.

Mary was just getting up from her chair after turning off the *tridi.* She was now bending over to pull a drawer from the wall. He saw that she was getting out their nightclothes. And, as he had for many a night now, he felt sick in his stomach.

Mary turned and saw his face.

"What's the matter?" she said.

"Nothing."

She walked across the room (only a few steps to traverse the length of the chamber, reminding him of how many steps he could take when he was on the Preserve). She handed him a crumpled-up mass of tissue-thin garments and said, "I don't think Olaf had them cleaned. It's not his fault, though. The deionizer isn't working. He left a note saying he called a technician. But you know how long it takes them to fix anything."

"I'll fix it myself, when I get time," he said. He sniffed at the nightclothes. "Great Sigmen! How long has the cleaner been out?"

"Ever since you left," she said.

"How that man does sweat!" Hal said. "He must be in a perpetual state of terror. No wonder! Old Olvegssen scares me, too."

Mary's face became red. "I have prayed and prayed that you wouldn't curse," she said. "When are you going to quit that unreal habit? Don't you know? . . ."

"Yes," he said, interrupting harshly, "I know that every time I take the Forerunner's name in vain, I delay Timestop just that much more. So what?"

Mary stepped back from the loudness of his voice and the curl of his lip.

" 'So what?' " she repeated incredulously. "Hal, you can't mean it?"

"No, of course I don't mean it!" he said, breathing heavily. "Of course I don't! How could I? It's just that I get so mad at your continual reminding me of my faults."

"The Forerunner himself said we must always remind our brother of his unrealities."

"I'm not your brother. I'm your husband," he said. "Though there are plenty of times, such as now, when I wish I weren't."

Mary lost the prim and reproving look, tears filled her eyes, and her lips and chin shook.

"For Sigmen's sake," he said. "Don't cry."

"How can I help it," she sobbed, "when my own husband, my own flesh and blood, united to me by the Real Sturch, heaps abuse on my head? And I have done nothing to deserve it."

"Nothing except turn me in to the *gapt* every chance you get," he said. He turned away from her and pulled the bed down from the wall.

"I suppose the bedclothes will stink of Olaf and his fat wife, too," he said.

He picked up a sheet, smelled it, and said, "Augh!" He tore off the other sheets and threw them on the floor. With them went his nightclothes.

"To H with them! I'm sleeping in my clothes. You call yourself a wife? Why didn't you take our stuff to our neighbor's and get them cleaned there?"

"You know why," she said. "We don't have the money to pay them for the use of their cleaner. If you'd get a higher M.R., then we could afford it."

"How can I get a higher M.R. when you babble to the *gapt* every time I commit a little indiscretion?"

"Why, that's not *my* fault!" she said indignantly. "What kind of Sigmenite would I be if I lied to the good *abba* and told him you deserved a better M.R.? I couldn't live with myself after that, knowing that I had been so grossly unreal and that the Forerunner was watching me. Why, when I'm with the *gapt,* I can feel the invisible eyes of Isaac Sigmen burning into me, reading my every thought. I couldn't! And you should be ashamed because you want me to!"

"H with you!" he said. He walked away and went into the unmentionable.

Inside the tiny room, he shed his clothes and stepped into the shower for the thirty-second fall of water allowed him. Then he stood in front of the blower until he was dried. Afterward, he brushed his teeth vigorously, as if he were trying to scour out the terrible words he had uttered. As usual, he was beginning to feel the shame of what he had said. And with it the fear of what Mary would tell the *gapt,* what he would tell the *gapt,* and what would happen afterward. It was possible that his M.R. would be so devaluated that he would be fined. If that happened, then his budget, strained as it was, would burst. And he would be more in debt than ever, not to mention that he would be passed over when the next promotion time came.

Thinking this, he put his clothes back on and left the little room. Mary brushed by him on her way into the unmentionable. She looked surprised on seeing him dressed, then she stopped and said, "Oh, that's right! You did throw the night-things on the floor! Hal, you can't mean it!"

"Yes, I do," he said. "I'm not sleeping in those sweaty things of Olaf's."

"Please, Hal," she said. "I wish you wouldn't use that word. You know that I can't stand vulgarity."

"I beg your pardon," he said. "Would you rather I used the Icelandic or Hebrew word for it? In either language, the word stands for the same vile human excretion: sweat!"

Mary put her hands to her ears, ran into the unmentionable, and slammed the door behind her.

He threw himself down on the thin mattress and put his arm over his eyes so the light would not get into them. In five minutes, he heard the door open (it was beginning to need oiling but would not get it until their budget and that of the Olaf Marconis could afford to buy the lubricant). And if his M.R. went down, the Marconis might petition to move into another apartment. If they could find one, then another, even more objectionable couple (probably one that had just been elevated from a lower professional class) would move in with them.

Oh, Sigmen! he thought. *Why can't I be content with things as they are? Why can't I accept reality fully? Why must I have so much of the Backrunner in me? Tell me, tell me!*

It was Mary's voice he heard as she settled into bed beside him. "Hal, surely you aren't going to stick to this *unshib?*"

"What *unshib?*" he said, though he knew what she meant.

"Sleeping in your dayclothes."

"Why not?"

"Hal!" she said. "You know very well why not!"

"No, I don't," he replied. He removed his arm from his eyes and stared into total blackness. She had, as prescribed, turned off the light before getting into bed.

Her body, if unclothed, would gleam white in the light of lamp or moon, he thought. *Yet, I have never seen her body, never seen her even half-undressed. Never seen any woman's body except for that picture that man in Berlin showed me. And I, after one half-hungry, half-horrified look, ran as swiftly as I could. I wonder if the Uzzites found him soon after and did to him whatever they do to men who pervert reality so hideously.*

So hideously . . . yet, he could see the picture as if it were before his eyes now in the full light of Berlin. And he could see the man who was trying to sell it to him, a tall, good-looking youth with blond hair and broad shoulders, speaking the Berliner variety of Icelandic.

White flesh gleaming . . .

Mary had been silent for several minutes, but he could hear her breathing. Then, "Hal, haven't you done enough since you came home? Must you make me tell the *gapt* even more?"

"And just what else have I done?" he asked fiercely. Nevertheless, he smiled slightly, for he was determined to make her speak plainly, to come out and ask. Not that she ever would, but he was going to get her to come as close as she was capable.

"That's just it, you haven't done anything," she whispered.

"Now what do you mean?"

"You know."

"No, I don't."

"The night before you left for the Preserve, you said you were too tired. That's no real excuse, but I didn't say anything to the *gapt* about it because you had fulfilled your weekly duty. But you've been gone two weeks, and now—"

"Weekly duty!" he said loudly, resting on one elbow. "Weekly duty! Is that what you think of it?"

"Why, Hal," she said with a surprised note. "What else am I to think?"

Groaning, he lay back down and stared into the dark.

"What's the use?" he said. "Why, why should we? Nine years we've been married; we've had no children; we never will. I've even petitioned for a divorce. So why should we continue to perform like a couple of robots on *tridi?*"

Mary's breath sucked in, and he could imagine the horror on her face.

After a moment which seemed to bulge with her shock, she said, "We must because we must. What else can we do? Surely, you're not suggesting that? . . ."

"No, no," he said quickly, thinking of what would happen if she told their *gapt*. Other things he could get away with, but any hint on her part that her husband was refusing to carry out the specific command of the Forerunner . . . He did not dare to think about that. At least, he now had prestige as a university teacher and a *puka* with some room in it and a chance to advance. But not if . . .

"Of course not," he said. "I know we must try to have children, even if we seem doomed not to."

"The doctors say there's nothing physically wrong with either of us," she said for perhaps the thousandth time in the past five years. "So, one of us must be thinking against reality, denying with his body the true future. And I know that it can't be me. It couldn't be!"

" 'The dark self hides overmuch from the bright self,' " said Hal, quoting *The Western Talmud*. " 'The Backrunner in us trips us, and we know it not.' "

There was nothing that so infuriated Mary, herself always quoting, as to have Hal do the same. But now, instead of beginning a tirade, she cried, "Hal, I'm scared! Do you realize that in another year our time will be up? That we'll go before the Uzzites for another test? And, if we fail, if they find out that one of us is denying the future to our children . . . they made it clear what would happen!"

Artificial insemination by a donor was adultery. Cloning had been forbidden by Sigmen because it was an abomination.

For the first time that evening, Hal felt a sympathy with her. He knew the same terror that was making her body quiver and shake the bed.

But he could not allow her to know it, for then she would break up completely, as she had several times in the past. He would be all night putting the pieces back together and making them stick.

"I don't think there is too much to worry about," he said. "After all, we are highly respected and much needed professionals. They're not about to waste our education and talents by sending us to H. I think that if you don't get pregnant, they'll give us an extension. After all, they do have precedent and authority. The Forerunner himself said that every case should be considered in its context, not judged by an absolute rule. And we—"

"And how often is a case judged by the context?" she said shrilly. "How often? You know as well as I do that the absolute rule is always applied!"

"I don't know any such thing," he replied soothingly. "How naïve can you get? If you go by what the truecasters say, yes. But I've heard some things about the hierarchy. I know that such things as blood relationship, friendship, prestige, and wealth, or usefulness to the Sturch, can make for a relaxation of the rules."

Mary sat upright in bed.

"Are you trying to tell me that the Urielites can be bribed?" she said in a shocked tone.

"I would never ever say that to anybody," he said. "And I will swear by Sigmen's lost hand that I did not mean even to hint at such a vile unreality. No, I am just saying that usefulness to the Sturch sometimes results in leniency or another chance."

"Who do you know to help us?" said Mary, and Hal smiled in the darkness. Mary could be shocked by his outspokenness, but she was practical and would not hesitate to use any means to get them out of their predicament.

There was silence for a few minutes. Mary was breathing hard, like a cornered animal.

Finally, he said, "I don't really know anybody with influence except Olvegssen. And he's been making remarks about my M.R., though he does praise my work."

"See! That M.R.! If you'd only make an effort, Hal . . ."

"If only you weren't so eager to downgrade me," he said bitterly.

"Hal, I can't help it if you go along so easily with unreality! I don't like what I have to do, but it's my duty! You're even making a misstep by reproaching me for what I have to do. Another black mark——"

"Which you will be forced to repeat to the *gapt.* Yes, I know. Let's not go into that again for the ten thousandth time."

"You brought it up," she said righteously.

"That seems to be all we have to talk about."

She gasped, and then she said, "It wasn't always that way."

"No, not for the first year of our marriage. But since then——"

"Whose fault is that?" she cried.

"That's a good question. But I don't think we should go into it. It might be dangerous."

"What do you mean?"

"I don't care to discuss it."

He was himself surprised at what he had said. What did he mean? He did not know; he had spoken, not with his intellect but with his whole being. Had the Backrunner in him made him say that?

"Let's get to sleep," he said. "Tomorrow changes the face of reality."

"Not before——" she said.

"Before what?" he replied wearily.

"Don't play *shib* with me," she said. "This is what started the whole thing. You trying to . . . put off your . . . duty."

"My duty," said Hal. "The *shib* thing to do. Of course."

"Don't talk like that," she said. "I don't want you to do it just because it's your duty. I want you to do it because you love me, as you are enjoined to do. Also, because you *want* to love me."

"I am enjoined to love all of mankind," said Hal. "But I notice that I am expressly forbidden to perform my duty with anyone but my realistically bound wife."

Mary was so shocked that she could not reply, and she turned her back to him. But he, knowing that he was doing it as much to punish her and himself as doing what he should, reached out for her. From then on, having made the formal opening statement, everything was ritualized. This time, unlike some times in the past, everything was executed step by step, the words and actions, as specified by the Forerunner in *The Western Talmud*. Except for one detail: Hal was still wearing his dayclothes. This, he had decided, could be forgiven, for it was the spirit, not the letter, that counted, and what was the difference whether he wore the thick street garments or the bulky nightclothes? Mary, if she had noticed the error, had said nothing about it.

3

AFTERWARD, lying on his back, staring into the darkness, Hal thought as he had many a time before. What was it that cut through his abdomen like a broad, thick steel plate and seemed to sever his torso from his hips? He was excited, in the beginning. He knew he must be because his heart beat fast, he breathed hard. Yet, he could not—really—feel anything. And when the moment came —which the Forerunner called the time of generation of potentiality, the fulfillment and actualization of reality—Hal experienced only a mechanical reaction. His body carried out its prescribed function, but he felt nothing of that ecstasy which the Forerunner had described so vividly. A zone of unfeeling, a nerve-chilling area, a steel plate, cut through him. He felt nothing except the jerkings of his body, as if an electrical needle were stimulating his nerves at the same time it numbed them.

This was wrong, he told himself. Or was it? Could it be that the Forerunner was mistaken? After all, the Forerunner was a man superior to the rest of humanity. Perhaps, he had been gifted enough to experience such exquisite reactions and had not realized that the remainder of mankind did not share his good fortune.

But no, that could not be, if it were true—and

perish the thought that it could not be—that the Fore-runner could see into every man's mind.

Then, Hal himself was lacking, he alone of all the disciples of the Real Sturch.

Or was he alone? He had never discussed his feelings with anyone. To do so was—if not unthinkable —undoable. It was obscene, unrealistic. He had never been told by his teachers not to discuss the matter; they had not had to tell him, for Hal knew without being told.

Yet, the Forerunner had described what his reactions should be.

Or had he done so directly? When Hal considered that section of *The Western Talmud* which was read only by engaged and married couples, he saw that the Forerunner had not actually depicted a physical state. His language had been poetical (Hal knew what poetical meant, for as a linguist, he had access to various works of literature forbidden to others), metaphorical, even metaphysical. Couched in terms which, analyzed, were seen to have little relation to reality.

Forgive me, Forerunner, thought Hal. *I meant that your words were not a scientific description of the actual electrochemical processes of the human nervous system. Of course, they apply directly on a higher level, for reality has many planes of phenomena.*

Subrealistic, realistic, pseudorealistic, surrealistic, superrealistic, retrorealistic.

No time for theology, he thought, *no wish to make my mind whirl again tonight as on many nights with the unsolvable, unanswerable. The Forerunner knew, but I can't.*

All he knew now was that he was not in phase with the world line; had not been, possibly never would be. He teetered on the brink of unreality every waking moment. And that was not good—the Back-runner would get him, he'd fall into the Forerunner's brother's evil hands ...

Hal Yarrow woke suddenly as the morning clarion rang through the apartment. For a moment, he was confused, the world of his dream meshing with his waking world.

Then, he rolled out of bed and stood up, looking down at Mary. She, as always, slept on through the first call, loud as it was, because it was not for her. In fifteen minutes, the second blast of bugles over the *tridi* would come, the women's call. By then he must be washed, shaved, dressed, and on his way. Mary would have fifteen minutes to get herself on the road; ten minutes later, the Olaf Marconis would enter from their night's work and prepare to sleep and live in this narrow world until the Yarrows returned.

Hal was even quicker than usual because he still wore his dayclothes. He relieved himself, washed his face and hands, rubbed cream over his face stubble, wiped off the loosened hairs (someday, if he ever rose to the rank of a hierarch, he would wear a beard, like Sigmen), combed his hair, and he was out of the unmentionable.

After stuffing the letters he'd received the previous night into his traveling bag, he started toward the door. Then, impelled by an unexpected and unanalyzable feeling, he turned and went back to the bed and stooped over to kiss Mary. She did not wake up, and he felt regret—for a second—because she had not known what he had done. This act was no duty, no requirement. It had come from the dark depths, where there must also be light. Why had he done it? Last night, he had thought he hated her. Now . . .

She could not help doing what she did any more than he. That, of course, was no excuse. Every self was responsible for its own destiny; if anything good or bad happened to a self, then only one person had caused that happening.

He amended his thought. He and Mary were the generators of their own misery. But not consciously so. Their bright selves did not want their love to be wrecked; it was their dark selves—the deep-down, crouching, horrible Backrunner in them—that was causing this.

Then, as he stood by the doorway, he saw Mary open her eyes and look, somewhat confusedly, at him. And, instead of returning to kiss her again, he hastily stepped into the hallway. He was in a panic, fearing that she might call him back and begin the whole dreary and nerve-racking scene again. Not until later did he realize that he had not had a chance to tell Mary that he would be on his way to Tahiti that very morning. Oh well, he was spared another scene.

By then, the hallway was crowded with men on their way to work. Many, like Hal, were dressed in the loose plaids of the professionals. Others wore the green and scarlet of university teachers.

Hal, of course, spoke to each one.

"Good future to you, Ericssen!"

"Sigmen smile, Yarrow!"

"Did you have a bright dream, Chang?"

"*Shib,* Yarrow! Straight from truth itself."

"Shalom, Kazimuru."

"Sigmen smile, Yarrow!"

Then Hal stood by the lift doors while a keeper, on duty at this level in the morning because of the crowd, arranged the priority of their descent. Once out of the tower, Hal stepped onto a series of belts with increasingly swift speed until he was on the express, the middle belt. Here he stood, pressed in by the bodies of men and women but at ease because they belonged to his class. Ten minutes of travel, and he began to work his way through the crowd from belt to belt. Five minutes later, he stepped off onto the sidewalk and walked into the cavernous entrance of Pali No. 16, University of Sigmen City.

Inside, he had to wait, though not for long, until the keeper had ushered him into the lift. Then, he went straight up on the express to the thirtieth level. Usually, when he got out of the lift, he went directly to his own office to deliver his first lecture of the day, an undergraduate course which went out over *tridi*. Today, Hal headed for the dean's office.

On the way, craving a cigarette and knowing that he could not smoke it in Olvegssen's presence, he stopped to light one and to breathe in the delicious ginseng smoke. He was standing outside the door of an elementary class in linguistics and could hear snatches of Keoni Jerahmeel Rasmussen's lecture.

"*Puka* and *pali* were originally words of the primitive Polynesian inhabitants of the Hawaiian Islands. The English-speaking people who later colonized the islands adopted many terms from the Hawaiian language; *puka,* meaning hole, tunnel, or cave, and *pali,* meaning cliff, were among the most popular.

"When the Hawaiian-Americans repopulated North America after the Apocalyptic War, these two terms were still being used in the original sense. But, about fifty years ago, the two words changed their meanings. *Puka* came to be applied to the small apartments allotted to the lower classes, obviously in a derogatory sense. Later, the term spread to the upper classes. However, if you are a hierach, you live in an apartment; if you belong to any class below the hierarchy, you live in a *puka.*

"*Pali,* which meant cliff, was applied to the skyscrapers or to any huge building. It, unlike *puka,* also retains its original meaning."

Hal finished his cigarette, dropped it in an ashtray, and walked on down the hall to the dean's office. There he found Doctor Bob Kafziel Olvegssen sitting behind his desk.

Olvegssen, the senior, spoke first, of course. He had a slight Icelandic accent.

"Aloha, Yarrow. And what are you doing here?"

"Shalom, *abba.* I beg your pardon for appearing before you without an invitation. But I had to arrange several matters before I left."

Olvegssen, a gray-haired middle-aged man of seventy, frowned.

"Left?"

Hal took the letter from his suitcase and handed it to Olvegssen.

"You may process it yourself later, of course. But I can save you valuable time by telling you it's another order to make a linguistic investigation."

"You just got back from one!" said Olvegssen. "How can they expect me to run this college efficiently and to the glory of the Sturch if they continually drag my staff away on wild word chases?"

"You're surely not criticizing the Urielites?" said Hal, not without a touch of malice. He did not like his superior, try though he had to overcome this unrealistic thinking on his part.

"Harumph! Of course not! I am incapable of doing so, and I resent your imputation that I might be!"

"Your pardon, *abba*," said Hal. "I would not dream of hinting at such a thing."

"When must you leave?" said Olvegssen.

"On the first coach. Which, I believe, takes off in an hour."

"And you will return?"

"Only Sigmen knows. When my investigation and the report are finished."

"Report to me at once when you return."

"I beg your pardon again, but I can't do that. My M.R. will be long overdue by then, and I am compelled to clear that out of the way before I do anything else. That may take hours."

Olvegssen scowled and said, "Yes, your M.R. You didn't do so well on your last, Yarrow. I trust your next shows some improvement. Otherwise . . ."

Suddenly, Hal felt hot all through his body, and his legs quivered.

"Yes, *abba?*"

His own voice sounded weak and distant.

Olvegssen made a steeple of his hands and looked at Yarrow over the tip.

"Much as I would regret it, I would be forced to

take action. I can't have a man with a low M.R. on my staff. I'm afraid that I . . . "

There was a long silence. Hal felt the sweat trickling down from his armpits and the beads forming on his forehead and upper lip. He knew that Olvegssen was purposely hanging him in suspense, and he did not want to ask him anything. He did not want to give the smug gray-haired *gimel* the satisfaction of hearing him speak. But he did not dare seem to be uninterested. And, if he did not say anything, he knew that Olvegssen would only smile and dismiss him.

"What, *abba?*" said Hal, striving to keep a choking sound from his voice.

"I'm very much afraid that I could not even allow myself the leniency of merely demoting you to secondary school teaching. I would like to be merciful. But mercy in your case might only be enforcing unreality. And I could not endure the possibility of that. No . . ."

Hal swore at himself because he could not control his trembling.

"Yes, *abba?*"

"I am very much afraid that I would have to ask the Uzzites to look into your case."

"No!" said Hal loudly.

"Yes," said Olvegssen, still speaking behind the steeple of his hands. "It would pain me to do that, but it would be *unshib* not to. Only by seeking their help could I dream correctly."

He broke the steeple of his hands, swung around in his chair so his profile was to Hal, and said, "However, there is no reason that I should have to take such steps, is there? After all, you and you alone are responsible for whatever happens to you. Therefore, you've nobody to blame but yourself."

"So the Forerunner has revealed," said Hal. "I will see that you are not pained, *abba*. I will make certain that my *gapt* has no reason to give me a low M.R."

"Very good," said Olvegssen as if he did not believe it. "I will not hold you up by examining your letter, for I should have a duplicate in today's mail. Aloha, my son, and good dreaming."

"See real, *abba*," said Hal, and he turned and left. In a daze of terror, he scarcely knew what he was doing. Automatically, he traveled to the port and there went through the process of obtaining priority for his trip. His mind still refused to function clearly when he got onto the coach.

Half an hour later, he got off at the port of LA and went to the ticket office to confirm his seat on the coach to Tahiti.

As he stood in the ticket line, he felt a tap on his shoulder.

He jumped, and then he turned to apologize to the person behind.

He felt his heart hammer as if it would batter through his chest.

The man was a squat broad-shouldered potbellied fellow in a loose, jet black uniform. He wore a tall, conical, shiny black hat with a narrow rim, and on his chest was the silvery figure of the angel Uzza.

The officer leaned forward to examine the Hebrew numbers on the lower rim of the winged foot Hal wore on his chest. Then he looked at a paper in his hand.

"You're Hal Yarrow, *shib*," said the Uzzite. "Come with me."

Afterward, Hal thought that one of the strangest aspects of the business was his lack of terror. Not that he had not been scared. It was just that the fear was pushed far down into a corner of his mind while the greater part devoted itself to considering the situation and how to get out of it. The vagueness and confusion that had filled him during his interview with Olvegssen and that had lasted long afterward now seemed to dissolve. He was left cold and quick-thinking; the world was clear and hard.

Perhaps, it was because the threat given by Olvegssen was distant and uncertain, whereas being taken into custody by the Uzzites was immediate and certainly dangerous.

He was taken to a small car on a strip by the ticket building. Here he was ordered into the seat. The Uzzite with him also got in, and he set the controls for his destination. The car rose vertically to about five hundred meters and then shot, sirens screaming, toward its destination. Hal, though not in a humorous mood, could not help reflecting that cops had not changed in the last thousand years. Even though no emergency warranted, the guardians of the law must make noise.

Within two minutes, the car had entered a port of a building at the twentieth level. Here the Uzzite, who had spoken not a word to Hal since the initial conversation, gestured to him to get out. Hal had not said anything either because he knew that it would be useless.

The two walked up a ramp and then through many corridors filled with hurrying people. Hal tried to keep the route straight just in case he was able to escape. He knew that flight was ridiculous, that he could not possibly get away. Also, he had no reason as yet to think that he would be in a situation where running was the only way out.

Or so he hoped.

Finally, the Uzzite stopped before an office door which bore no legend. He jerked his thumb at it, and Hal walked in ahead of him. He found himself in an anteroom; a female secretary sat behind a desk.

"Angel Patterson reporting," said the Uzzite. "I have Hal Yarrow, Professional LIN–56327."

The secretary relayed the information through a speaker, and a voice came from the wall telling the two to enter.

The secretary pressed a button, and the door swung open.

Hal, still in the lead, walked in.

He was in a room large by his standards, larger even than his classroom or his whole *puka* in Sigmen City. At its far end was a huge desk whose top curved like a crescent or a pair of sharp horns. Behind it sat a man, and the sight of the man shattered Hal's calm composure. He had expected a *gapt* of high rank, a man dressed in black and wearing a conical hat.

But this man was not an Uzzite. He was clad in flowing purple robes with a cowl over his head, and on his chest was a large golden Hebrew *L*, the *lamedh*. And he had a beard.

He was among the highest of the high, a Urielite. Hal had seen his kind only a dozen times in his life and only once before in the flesh.

He thought, Great Sigmen, what have I done? I'm doomed, doomed!

The Urielite was a very tall man, almost half a head higher than Hal. His face was long, his cheekbones protruding, his nose large, narrow, and curved, his lips thin, and his eyes pale blue with a slight internal epicanthic fold.

Behind Hal, the Uzzite said in a very low voice, "Halt, Yarrow! Stand at attention! Do everything the Sandalphon Macneff says, without hesitation and with no false moves."

Hal, who would not have thought of disobeying, nodded his head.

Macneff looked at Yarrow for at least a minute, meanwhile stroking his bushy brown beard.

Then, after making Hal sweat and quiver inwardly, Macneff finally spoke. His voice was surprisingly deep for such a thin-necked man.

"Yarrow, how would you like to leave this life?"

4

AFTERWARD, Hal had time to thank Sigmen that he had not followed his impulse.

Instead of becoming paralyzed with terror, he had considered whirling swiftly and attacking the Uzzite. The officer, though he wore no visible arms, undoubtedly had a gun in a holster under his robes. If Hal could knock him out and get the weapon, he might be able to take Macneff as a hostage. With him as a shield, Hal could flee.

Where?

He had no idea. To Israel or the Malay Federation? Both were a long way off, though distance meant little if he could steal or commandeer a ship. Even if he succeeded in doing that, he had no chance of getting past the antimissile stations. Unless he could fool the guards, and he did not know enough of military usage or codes to do that.

Meanwhile, thinking of the possibilities, he felt the impulse die. It would be more intelligent to wait until he found out what he was accused of. Perhaps, he could prove that he was innocent.

Macneff's thin lips curved slightly in a smile that Hal was to know well. He said, "That is good, Yarrow."

Hal did not know if he had been given an implication to speak, but he took a chance of not offending the Uriclite.

"What is good, Sandalphon?"

"That you turned red instead of pale. I am a reader of selves, Yarrow. I can see into a man within a few seconds after meeting him. And I saw that you were not ready to faint with terror, as many would have done if they had just heard my first words to you. No, you became flushed with the hot blood of aggressiveness. You were ready to deny, to argue, to fight against anything I might say.

"Now, some might say that that would not be a favorable reaction, that your attitude showed wrong thinking, a leaning toward unreality.

"But I say, *What is reality?* That was the question propounded by the Forerunner's evil brother in the great debate. The answer is the same, that only the real man can tell.

"I am real; otherwise, I would not be a Sandalphon. *Shib?*"

Hal, trying to keep from breathing noisily, nodded. He was thinking that Macneff must not be able to read as clearly as he thought he could, for he had said nothing about knowing Hal's first intention to resort to violence.

Or did Macneff know but was wise enough to forgive?

"When I asked you how you would like to leave this life," said Macneff, "I was not suggesting that you were a candidate for H."

He frowned, and he said, "Though your M.R. suggests that if you keep on your present level, you may soon be. However, I am certain that if you volunteer for what I propose, you will soon straighten out. You would then be in close contact with many *shib* men; you could not escape their influence. 'Reality breeds reality.' So said Sigmen.

"However, I may be rushing things. First, you must swear on this book"—he picked up a copy of *The Western Talmud*—"that nothing that we say in this office will be divulged to any person under any circumstances. You will die or undergo any torture before you betray the Sturch."

Hal put his left hand on the book (Sigmen used his left hand because of the early loss of his right), and he swore by the Forerunner and all the levels of reality that his lips would be locked forever. Otherwise, he cut himself off forever from any hope of the glory of seeing the Forerunner face to face and of some day having his own universe to rule.

Even as he swore, he began to feel guilty because he had thought of striking an Uzzite and using force on a Sandalphon. How could he have given in to his dark self so suddenly? Macneff was the living representative of Sigmen while Sigmen was voyaging through time and space to prepare the future for his disciples. To refuse to obey Macneff in any degree was to strike the Forerunner in the face, and that was a thing so terrible he could not bear to think of it.

Macneff put the book back on the desk, and he said, "First, I must tell you that your getting that order to investigate the word *woggle* in Tahiti was a mistake. Probably because certain departments of the Uzzites were not working as closely together as they should. The reason for the mistake is even now being researched, and effective measures will be taken to make sure similar errors do not occur in the future."

The Uzzite behind Hal sighed heavily, and Hal knew that he was not the only man in the room capable of feeling fear.

"One of the hierarchy noticed, while going over his reports, that you had applied for permission to travel to Tahiti. Knowing how high a security rating the island has, he investigated. As a result, we were able to intercept you. And I, after examining your record, concluded that you might be just the one we needed to fill a certain position on the ship."

By now, Macneff had walked from behind his desk and was pacing back and forth, his hands clasped behind him, his body stooped forward. Hal could see how pale yellow Macneff's skin was, much the same color as the elephant tusk Hal had once seen in the Museum of Extinct Animals. The purple of the cowl over his head brought out the sallowness.

"You will be asked to volunteer," said Macneff, "because we want none but the most dedicated men aboard. However, I hope you do join us, because I would feel uneasy about leaving on Earth any civilian who knew the existence and destination of the *Gabriel*. Not that I doubt your loyalty, but the Israeli spies are very clever, and they might trick you into revealing what you know. Or kidnap you and use drugs to make you talk. They are devoted followers of the Backrunner, those Israeli."

Hal wondered why the use of drugs by the Israeli was so unrealistic and by the Haijac Union so *shib*, but he forgot about that when he heard Macneff's next words.

"A hundred years ago, the first interstellar spaceship of the Union left Earth for Alpha Centaurus. About the same time, an Israeli ship left. Both returned in twenty years and reported they had found no habitable planets. A second Haijac expedition came back ten years after that and a second Israeli vessel twelve years after it. None found a star with any planets human beings could colonize."

"I never knew that," murmured Hal Yarrow.

"Both governments have kept the secret well from their people, though not from each other," said Macneff. "The Israeli, as far as we know, have sent no more interstellar craft out since the second one. The expense and time involved are astronomical. However, we sent a third vessel out, a much smaller and faster one than the first two. We have learned much about interstellar drives since a hundred years ago; that is all I can tell you about them.

"But the third ship came back several years ago and reported—"

"That it had found a planet on which human beings could live and which was already inhabited by sentient beings!" said Hal, forgetting in his enthusiasm that he had not been asked to speak.

Macneff stopped pacing to stare at Hal with his pale blue eyes.

"How did you know?" he said sharply.

"Forgive me, Sandalphon," said Hal. "But it was inevitable! Did not the Forerunner predict in his *Time and the World Line* that such a planet would be found? I believe it was on page five seventy-three!"

Macneff smiled and said, "I am glad that your scriptural lessons have left such an impression."

How could they not? Hal thought. Besides, they were not the only impressions. Pornsen, my *gapt,* whipped me because I had not learned my lessons well enough. He was a good impresser, that Pornsen. Was? Is! As I grew older and was promoted, so was he, always where I was. He was my *gapt* in the crêche. He was the dormitory *gapt* when I went to college and thought I was getting away from him. He is now my block *gapt.* He is the one responsible for my getting such low M.R.'s.

Swiftly came the revulsion, the protest. No, not he, for I, and I alone, am responsible for whatever happens to me. If I get a low M.R., I do so because I want it that way, or my dark self does. If I die, I die because I willed it so. So, forgive me, Sigmen, for the contrary-to-reality thoughts!

"Please pardon me again, Sandalphon," said Hal. "But did the expedition find any records of the Forerunner having been on this planet? Perhaps, even, though this is too much to wish, find the Forerunner himself?"

"No," said Macneff. "Though that does not mean that there may not be such records there. The expedition was under orders to make a swift survey of conditions and then to return to Earth. I can't tell you now the distance in light-years or what star this was, though you can see it with the naked eye at night in this hemisphere. If you volunteer, you will be told where you're going after the ship leaves. And it leaves very soon."

"You need a linguist?" said Hal.

"The ship is huge," said Macneff, "but the number of military men and specialists we are taking limits the linguists to one. We have considered several of your professionals because they were *lamedhians* and above suspicion. Unfortunately . . ."

Hal waited. Macneff paced some more, frowning. Then, he said, "Unfortunately, only one *lamedhian joat* exists, and he is too old for this expedition. Therefore—"

"A thousand pardons," said Hal. "But I have just thought of one thing. I am married."

"No problem at all," said Macneff. "There will be no women aboard the *Gabriel*. And, if a man is married, he will automatically be given a divorce."

Hal gasped, and he said, "A divorce?"

Macneff raised his hands apologetically and said, "You are horrified, of course. But, from our reading of *The Western Talmud*, we Urielites believe that the Forerunner, knowing this situation would arise, made reference to and provision for divorce. It's inevitable in this case, for the couple will be separated for, at the least, eighty objective years. Naturally, he couched the provision in obscure language. In his great and glorious wisdom, he knew that our enemies the Israelites must not be able to read therein what we planned."

"I volunteer," said Hal. "Tell me more, Sandalphon."

Six months later, Hal Yarrow stood in the observation dome of the *Gabriel* and watched the ball of Earth dwindle above him. It was night on this hemisphere, but the light blazed from the megalopolises of Australia, Japan, China, Southeast Asia, India, Siberia. Hal, the linguist, saw the glittering disks and necklaces in terms of the languages spoken therein. Australia, the Philippine Islands, Japan, and northern China were inhabited by those members of the Haijac Union that spoke American.

Southern China, all of southeast Asia, southern India, and Ceylon, these states of the Malay Federation spoke Bazaar.

Siberia spoke Icelandic.

Hal's mind turned the globe swiftly for him, and he visualized Africa, which used Swahili south of the Sahara Sea. All around the Mediterranean Sea, Asia Minor, northern India, and Tibet, Hebrew was the native tongue. In southern Europe, between the Israeli Republics and the Icelandic-speaking peoples of northern Europe, was a thin but long stretch of territory called March. This was no man's land, disputed by the Haijac Union and the Israeli Republics, a potential source of war for the last two hundred years. Neither nation would give up their claim on it, yet neither wished to make any move that might lead to a second Apocalyptic War. So, for all practical purposes, it was an independent nation and by now had its own government (unrecognized outside its own borders). Its citizens spoke all of the world's surviving tongues, plus a new one called Lingo, a pidgin whose vocabulary was derived from the other six and whose syntax was so simple it could be contained on half a sheet of paper.

Hal saw in his mind the rest of Earth: Iceland, Greenland, the Caribbean Islands, and the eastern half of South America. Here the peoples spoke the tongue of Iceland because that island had gotten the jump on the Hawaiian-Americans who were busy resettling North America and the western half of South America after the Apocalyptic War.

Then there was North America, where American was the native speech of all except the twenty descendants of French-Canadians living on the Hudson Bay Preserve.

Hal knew that when that side of Earth rotated into the night zone, Sigmen City would blaze out into space. And, somewhere in that enormous light, was his apartment. But Mary would soon no longer be living there, for she would be notified in a few days that her husband had died in an accident. She would weep in private, he was sure, for she loved him in her frigid way, though in public she would be dry-eyed. Her friends and professional associates would sympathize with her, not because she had lost a beloved husband, but because she had been married to a man who thought unrealistically. If Hal Yarrow had been killed in a crash, he must have wanted it that way. There was no such thing as an "accident." Somehow, all the other passengers (also supposed to have died in this web of elaborate frauds to cover up the disappearance of the personnel of the *Gabriel*) had simultaneously "agreed" to die. And, therefore, being in disgrace, they would not be cremated and their ashes flung to the winds in public ceremony. No, the fish could eat their bodies for all the Sturch cared.

Hal felt sorry for Mary; he had a time keeping the tears from welling to his own eyes as he stood in the crowd in the observation dome.

Yet, he told himself, this was the best way. He and Mary would no longer have to tear and rend at each other; their mutual torture would be over. Mary was free to marry again, not knowing that the Sturch had secretly given her a divorce, thinking that death had dissolved her marriage. She would have a year in which to make up her mind, to choose a mate from a list selected by her *gapt*. Perhaps, the psychological barriers that had prevented her from conceiving Hal's child would no longer be present. Perhaps. Hal doubted if this happy event would occur. Mary was as frozen below the navel as he. No matter who the candidate for marriage selected by the *gapt* . . .

The *gapt*. Pornsen. He would no longer have to see that fat face, hear that whining voice . . .

"Hal Yarrow!" said the whining voice.

Slowly, icy yet burning, Hal turned.

There was the squat, loose-jowled, thick-lipped, vulture-nosed, narrow-eyed man smiling at him. Under the narrow-brimmed conical azure hat, gray-flecked black hair hung down to a high-ruffed black collar. The azure jacket fit snugly over a large paunch

—Pornsen had endured many a lecture from his superiors because of his overeating—and a broad blue belt held a metal clasp for the handle of his whip. The thick legs were enclosed in tight azure pants with a black stripe running vertically along the outer and inner sides and with azure knee-high boots. The feet, however, were so tiny they looked ridiculous. On the toes of each boot was a seven-sided mirror.

There were some dirty stories about the origin of the mirrors circulating among lower-class elements. Hal had once overheard one, and he still blushed whenever he recalled it.

"My beloved ward, my perennial gadfly," Pornsen whined. "I'd no idea that you would be on this glorious voyage. But I might've known! We seem to be bound by love. Sigmen himself must have foreseen it. Love to you, my ward."

"Sigmen love you, too," Hal said, and he coughed. "How wonderful to see your cherished self. I had thought we'd never see each other again."

5

THE *Gabriel* pointed toward her destination and, under one-gee acceleration, began to build toward her ultimate velocity, 33.1 percent of the speed of light. Meanwhile, all the personnel except those few needed to carry out the performance of the ship went into the suspensor. Here they would lie in suspended animation for many years. Some time later, after a check had been made of all automatic equipment, the crew would join the others. They would sleep while the *Gabriel*'s drive would increase the acceleration to a point which the unfrozen bodies of the personnel could not have endured. Upon reaching the desired speed, the automatic equipment would cut off the drive, and the silent but not empty vessel would hurl toward the star which was its journey's end.

Many years later, the photon-counting apparatus in the nose of the ship would determine that the star was close enough to actuate deceleration. Again, a force too strong for unfrozen bodies to endure would be applied. Then, after slowing the vessel considerably, the drive would adjust to a one-gee deceleration. And the crew would be automatically brought out of their suspended animation. These members would then unthaw the rest of the personnel. And, in the half-year left before reaching their destination, the men would carry out whatever preparations were needed.

Hal Yarrow was among the last to go into the sus-

pensor and among the first to come out. He had to
study the recordings of the language of the chief nation of Ozagen, Siddo. And, from the first, he faced
a difficult task. The expedition that had discovered
Ozagen had succeeded in correlating five thousand
Siddo words with an equal number of American
words. The description of the Siddo syntax was very
restricted. And, as Hal found out, obviously mistaken
in many cases.

This discovery caused Hal anxiety. His duty was to
write a school text and to teach the entire personnel
of the *Gabriel* how to speak Ozagen. Yet, if he used
all of the little means at his disposal, he would be in-
structing his students wrongly. Moreover, getting even
this across would be difficult.

For one thing, the organs of speech of the Ozagen
natives differed somewhat from Earthmen's; the
sounds made by these organs were, therefore, dissimi-
lar. It was true that they could be approximated, but
would the Ozagenians understand these approximations?

Another obstacle was the grammatical construction
of Siddo. Consider the tense system. Instead of inflect-
ing a verb or using an unattached particle to indicate
the past or future, Siddo used an entirely different
word. Thus, the masculine animate infinitive *dab-
humaksanigalu'ahai,* meaning *to live,* was, in the perfect tense, *ksu'u'peli'afo,* and, in the future, *mai'teipa.*
The same use of an entirely different word applied for
all the other tenses. Plus the fact that Siddo not only
had the normal (to Earthmen) three genders of masculine, feminine, and neuter, but the two extra of
inanimate and spiritual. Fortunately, gender was inflected, though the expression of it would be difficult
for anybody not born in Siddo. The system of indicating gender varied according to tense.

Other parts of speech—nouns, pronouns, adjectives-
adverbs, and conjunctions—operated under the same
system as the verbs. To confuse the use of the tongue,

different social classes quite often used different words to express the same meaning.

The writing of Siddo could only be compared to that of ancient Japanese. There was no alphabet; instead, ideograms, lines whose length, shape, and relative angle to each other were meaningful, were used. Signs accompanying each ideogram indicated the correct inflection of gender.

In the privacy of his study cubicle, Hal swore mildly by the lost right hand of Sigmen.

The captain of the first expedition had picked out the continent in the Ozagenian antipodes as his base for research. This happened to be occupied by natives who spoke the most difficult language (for Earthmen) to master. If he had chosen the other continent in the northern hemisphere, he could have had (rather, his linguist could have had) forty different tongues to choose from, some of them comparatively easy in their syntax and with short words. That is, they were if Hal could believe the random sample of them that the linguist had taken.

Siddo, the land mass in the southern hemisphere, was about the size, though not the shape, of Africa and was separated from the other by ten thousand miles of ocean. If the wog geologists were correct, it had once been part of a Gondwanaland, but then it had drifted away. Evolution had then taken a somewhat different path from that on the other continent. Whereas the other continent had been dominated by insects and their distant cousins, the endoskeletal pseudoarthropods, this land mass had been very hospitable to mammals. Though, Sigmen knew, there was an abundance of insect life on it.

The sentient species on Abaka'a'tu, the northern land mass, had been, until five hundred years ago, the wogglebug. On Siddo it had been a remarkably human-looking animal. There *Homo ozagen* had developed a culture at a stage analogous to that of ancient Egypt or Babylon. And then almost all the humans, civilized or savage, had perished.

This had happened only a thousand years before the first wogglebug Columbus had landed on their great continent. At the time of the discovery and for two centuries after, the wogs had presumed that the indigenes were extinct. But, as the wog colonists began penetrating the jungles and mountains of the interior, they encountered a few small groups of humanoids. These had retreated into the wilderness, where they could hide as successfully as the African pygmies had hidden before the great rain forests were cut down. It was estimated that there might be a thousand, maybe two thousand, scattered over an area of 100,000 square kilometers.

A few specimens, all males, had been captured by the wogs. Before releasing them, the wogs had learned their languages. They'd also tried to find out why the humanoids had so suddenly and mysteriously disappeared. Their informants had explanations, but these were contradictory and of obvious mythical origin. They just did not know the truth, though it might be concealed in their myths. Some explained the catastrophe as a plague sent by the Great Goddess or All-Mother. Others said she had sent a horde of demons to wipe out her worshippers because they had sinned against her laws. One story had it that she had shaken loose the stars so that they fell on all but a few of the people.

In any event, Yarrow did not have all the data he needed for his study. The linguist on the first expedition had had only eight months to gather his data, and a good part of that had been spent teaching several wogs American before he could really get started. The ship had stayed ten months on Ozagen, but for the first two months the crew had remained aboard while robots collected atmospheric and biota specimens, which were analyzed to make sure that the Terrans could venture forth without being poisoned or stricken by disease.

Despite all precautions, two had died of insect bites, one had been killed by a peculiar form of predator, and then half of the personnel had been stricken with a very debilitating but not fatal disease. This was caused by a bacterium which was innocuous to the natives but which had mutated in the bodies of its non-Ozagen hosts.

Fearing that other diseases might occur, and being under orders to make only a survey, not a thorough exploration, the captain had ordered a return to home. The personnel had been quarantined for a long time on a satellite station before they were allowed to touch Earth again. The linguist had died a few days after the landing.

While the second ship was being built, a vaccine for the disease was prepared. And other collected bacteria and viri were tested on animals and then on human beings who had been sent to H. This had resulted in a number of vaccines, some of which had made the crew of the *Gabriel* sick.

For some reason known only to the hierarchy, the captain of the first ship had been disgraced. Hal thought that this could be because he had failed to get samples of the blood of the natives. From what little Hal had learned, and this was only through some rumors, the wogs had just refused to allow their blood to be taken. Perhaps, this was because the suspicious behavior of the Haijacs had infected the wogs. When the Terrestrial scientists had then asked for corpses to dissect—for purely scientific reasons, of course—the wogs had again refused. All of their dead, they claimed, were cremated and their ashes strewn on the fields. It was true that they were often dissected by their own doctors before cremation, but it was part of their religion that this be done ritually. And a wog physician-priest had to perform it.

The captain had considered abducting some wogs just before the takeoff. But he'd felt that it wouldn't be wise to antagonize them at this time. He knew that a second expedition in a much larger vessel would be sent to Ozagen after he'd made his report. If its biologists couldn't talk the wogs into supplying blood samples, then force would be used.

While the *Gabriel* was being built, a top-echelon linguist had read the notes and listened to the recordings of his predecessor. But he'd spent too much time in trying to make comparisons with various aspects of Siddo to those of Terran languages, dead or alive. Where he should have been setting up a system by which the crew could learn Siddo in the quickest manner, he'd indulged his scholarly inclinations. Maybe this was the reason he wasn't going on the ship. Hal didn't know. He'd been given no explanation of why he was a last-minute substitute.

So Hal swore and bent to his work. He listened to the sounds of Siddo and studied their waveforms on the oscilloscope. He labored at reproducing them with his un-Ozagenian tongue, lips, teeth, palate, and larynx. He worked on a Siddo-American dictionary, an essential which his predecessor had somewhat neglected.

Unfortunately, before he or any of his crew mates could become fully conversant in Siddo, its native speakers would be dead.

Hal worked six months, long after all but the skeleton crew had gone into the suspensor. What annoyed him most about the project was the presence of Pornsen. The *gapt* would have gone into deep freeze, but he had to stay awake to watch Hal, to correct any unreal behavior on his part. The only redeeming feature was that Hal did not have to talk to Pornsen unless he felt like it, because he could use the urgency of his work as an excuse. But he tired of it after a while and of the loneliness. Pornsen was the most available human being to talk to, so Hal talked to him.

Hal Yarrow was also among the first to come out of the suspensor. This, he was told, was forty years later. Intellectually, he accepted the statement. But he never really believed it. There was no change in the physical appearance of himself or his shipmates. And the only change outside the ship was in the increased brightness of the star that was their destination.

Eventually, the star became the brightest object in the universe. Then, the planets circling it became visible. Ozagen, the fourth from the star, loomed. Approximately the size of Earth, it looked—from a distance—exactly like Earth. The *Gabriel* slipped into orbit after feeding data into the computer. For fourteen days, the vessel whirled around the planet while observations were made from the *Gabriel* itself and from gigs which descended into the atmosphere and even made several landings.

Finally, Macneff told the captain to take the *Gabriel* down.

Slowly, using immense quantities of fuel because of her vast mass, the *Gabriel* eased into the atmosphere and toward Siddo, the capital city, on the central-eastern coast. It settled gently as snowfall toward an open stretch in a park in the heart of the city. Park? The entire city was a park; the trees were so plentiful that from the air Siddo looked as if only a few people lived in it, not the estimated quarter of a million. There were many buildings, some ten stories high, but they were so widely separated they did not make an aggregate impression. The streets were wide, but they were overgrown by a grass so tough it could withstand any amount of wear. Only on the busy harbor front did Siddo resemble anything like an Earth city. Here the buildings were clustered close together, and the water was packed with sail ships and paddle-wheeled steamboats.

Down came the *Gabriel* while the crowd that had gathered below it ran to the borders of the meadow. Its colossal gray bulk settled upon the grass and at once began imperceptibly sinking into the soil. The Sandalphon, Macneff, ordered the main port opened. And, followed close behind by Hal Yarrow, who was to assist him if he stumbled in his speech to the welcoming delegation, Macneff stepped out into the open air of the first habitable planet discovered by Earthmen.

Like Columbus, thought Hal. *Will the story be the same?*

Afterward, the Terrans discovered that the mighty vessel lay at right angles across and above two underground steam-railroad tunnels. There was, however, no danger of their collapsing. The holes went through solid rock with six meters of another stratum of rock and twenty meters of dirt above it. Moreover, the ship was so long that most of its weight pressed on the area outside the tunnels. After determining this, the captain decided that the *Gabriel* should stay where it was.

From sunrise to sunset, its personnel ventured among the natives, learning all they could of their language, customs, history, biology, and other things, data which the first expedition had failed to get.

To make sure that the wogs didn't think the Terrans were suspiciously eager to get blood samples, Hal didn't bring up the matter for six weeks. In the meantime he spent much time—with Pornsen usually present—with a native named Fobo. He was one of the two who had learned American and a little Icelandic during the first expedition. Though he didn't know any more of the former language than Hal knew of Siddo, he did know enough to speed up Hal's mastery of Siddo. Sometimes, they talked quite fluently, on a simple level, by mixing up the two tongues.

One of the things about which the Earthmen were covertly curious was the Ozagen technology. Logically, there was nothing to fear from them. As far as could be determined, the wogs had progressed no further than Earth's early-twentieth-century (A.D.) science. But the human beings had to make sure that what met the eye was all that was there. What if the wogs were hiding weapons of devastating power, waiting to catch the visitors unawares?

Missiles and atomic warheads were not to be feared. Obviously, Ozagen was not, as yet, capable of making these. But the wogs did seem to be very advanced in biological science. And this was to be dreaded as much as thermonuclear weapons. Moreover, even if disease was not used to attack the Earthmen, disease remained a deadly threat. What might be a nuisance to an Ozagenian with millennia of acquired immunity could be a swift death to a Terrestrial.

So—slow and cautious was the order. Find out everything possible. Gather data, correlate, interpret. Before beginning Project Ozagenocide, make sure that retaliation is impossible. *Make sure*.

Thus it was that four months after the appearance of the *Gabriel* above Siddo, two presumably friendly (to wogs) Terrans set out on a trip with two presumably friendly (to Terrans) wogglebugs. They were going to investigate the ruins of a city built two thousand years ago by now nearly extinct humanoids. They were inspired by a dream that had been dreamed on the planet Earth years before and light-years distant.

They rode in a vehicle fantastic to the human beings.

6 **苁**

THE motor hiccoughed, and the car jerked. The Ozagenian sitting on the right side of the rear seat leaned over and shouted something.

Hal Yarrow turned his head and yelled, "What?" He repeated in Siddo, " '*Abhudai'akhu?*' "

Fobo, sitting directly behind Hal, stuck his mouth against the Earthman's ear. He translated for Zugu, though his American sounded weird with its underlying trill and resonant approximations.

"Zugu says and emphasizes that you should pump that little rod to your right. It gives the . . . carburetor . . . more alcohol."

The antennae on Fobo's skullcap tickled Hal's ears. Hal spoke a word-sentence consisting of thirty syllables. This meant, roughly, "I thank you." It consisted initially of the verb used in the present masculine animate singular first person form. Attached to the verb was a syllable indicating freedom from obligation on the part of either the speaker or hearer, the inflected first person pronoun, another syllable indicating that the speaker acknowledged the hearer as most knowledgeable of the two, the third person masculine animate singular pronoun, and two syllables which, in their order of sequence, classified the whole present situation as semihumorous. Reversed in sequence, the classifier would indicate that the situation was serious.

"What did you say?" shouted Fobo, and Hal shrugged. He suddenly realized that he had forgotten a palatal click, the lack of which either changed the meaning of the phrase or else made it completely meaningless. In either case, he did not have the time or the will to repeat.

Instead, he worked the throttle as Fobo had directed. To do so, he had to lean across the *gapt,* sitting at his right.

"A thousand pardons!" Hal bellowed.

Pornsen did not look at Yarrow. His hands, lying on his lap, were locked together. The knuckles were white. Like his ward, he was having his first experience with an internal combustion motor. Unlike Hal, he was scared by the loud noise, the fumes, the bumps and bangs, and the idea of riding in a manually controlled ground vehicle.

Hal grinned. He loved this quaint car, which reminded him of the pictures in the history books of Earth's automobiles during the second decade of the twentieth century. It thrilled him to be able to twist the stiff-acting wheel and feel the heavy body of the vehicle obey his muscles. The banging of the four cylinders and the reek of burning alcohol excited him. As for the rough riding, that was fun. It was romantic, like putting out to sea in a sailboat—something else he hoped to do before he left Ozagen.

Also, though he would not admit it to himself, anything that scared Pornsen pleased him.

His pleasure ended. The cylinders popped, then sputtered. The car bucked and jerked and rolled to a stop. The two wogglebugs hopped over the side of the car (no doors) and raised the hood. Hal followed. Pornsen remained on the seat. He pulled a package of Merciful Seraphim (if angels smoked, they'd prefer Merciful Seraphim) out of his uniform pocket and lit one. His hands shook.

Hal noted it was the fourth he'd seen Pornsen smoking since morning prayers. If Pornsen wasn't careful, he'd be going over the quota allowed even first-class *gapts.* That meant that the next time Hal got into trouble, he could ask the *gapt* for help by reminding him . . . No! That was too shameful a thought to keep in his head. Definitely unreal, belonging only in a pseudofuture. He loved the *gapt* as the *gapt* loved him, and he should not be planning such an un-Sigmenlike path of behavior.

Yet, he thought, judging from the difficulties he'd been in so far, he could use some help from Pornsen.

Hal shook his head to clear himself of such thoughts and bent over the motor to watch Zugu work on it. Zugu seemed to know what he was doing. He should, since he was the inventor and builder of the only—as far as the Terrans knew—Ozagenian vehicle driven by an internal combustion motor.

Zugu used a wrench to unscrew a long narrow pipe from a round glass case. Hal remembered that this was a gravity feed system. The fuel ran from the tank into the glass case, which was a sediment chamber. From there it ran into the feed pipe, which in turn passed the fuel on to the carburetor.

Pornsen called harshly, "Beloved son, are we going to be stuck here all day?"

Though he wore the mask and goggles which the Ozagenians had given him as windbreakers, his tight lips were enough expression. It was evident that unless events improved, the *gapt* would turn in a report unfavorable to his ward.

The *gapt* had wanted to wait the two days that would be needed until he could requisition a gig. The trip to the ruins could then have been made in fifteen minutes, a soundless and comfortable ride through the air. Hal had argued that driving would give more valuable espionage in this heavily forested country than surveying from the air. That his superiors had agreed was another thing that had exasperated Pornsen. Where his ward went, he had to go.

So, he had sulked all day while the young Terran, coached by Zugu, wheeled the jalopy down the forest roads. The only time Pornsen spoke was to remind

Hal of the sacredness of the human self and to tell him to slow down.

Hal would reply, "Forgive me, cherished guardian," and would ease his foot off the accelerator. But, after a while, he would slowly press down. Once again, they would roar and leap down the rough dirt road.

Zugu unscrewed both ends of the pipe, stuck one end in his V-shaped mouth, and blew. Nothing, however, came out of the other end. Zugu shut his big blue eyes and puffed his cheeks out again. Nothing happened, except that his lightly tinged green face turned a dark olive. Then, he rapped the copper tubing against the hood and blew once more. Same result.

Fobo reached into a large leather pouch slung from a belt around his big belly. His finger and thumb came out, holding between them a tiny blue insect. Gently, he pushed the creature into one end of the pipe. After five seconds, a small red insect in a hurry dropped out of the other end. Behind it, hungrily crossing its mandibles, came the blue insect. Fobo deftly snared his pet and replaced it in the pouch. Zugu squashed the red bug beneath his sandal.

"Behold!" said Fobo. "An eater of alcohol! It lives in the fuel tank and imbibes freely and unmolested. It extracts the carbohydrates therein. A swimmer upon the golden seas of alcohol. What a life! But now and then it becomes too adventurous, travels into the sediment chamber, eats and devours the filter, and passes into the feedpipe. *See!* Zugu is even now replacing the filter. In a moment, we will be on our way down the road."

Fobo's breath had a strange and sickening odor. Hal wondered if the wog had been drinking liquor. He had never smelled it on anybody's breath before, so he had no experience to go on. But even the thought of it made Hal nervous. If the *gapt* knew a bottle was being passed back and forth in the rear seat, he would not allow Hal out of his sight for a minute.

The wogs climbed into the back of the car. "Let's go and depart!" said Fobo.

"Just a minute," said Pornsen in a low voice to Hal. "I think it's better that Zugu drive this thing."

"If you ask the wog to drive, he'll know you lack confidence in me, your fellow Terran," said Hal. "You wouldn't want him to think it was your belief that a wog is superior to a human being, would you?"

Pornsen coughed as if he had trouble swallowing Hal's remarks, then sputtered, "Of-of-of course not! Sigmen forbid! It was just that I had your welfare in mind. I thought you might be tired after the strain of piloting this primitive and dangerous contraption all day."

"Thank you for your love for me," said Hal. He grinned and added, "It is comforting to know you are always at my side, ready to direct me away from the peril of pseudofutures."

Pornsen said, "I have sworn by *The Western Talmud* to guide you through this life."

Chastened by the mention of the sacred book, Hal started the car. At first, he drove slowly enough to suit the *gapt*. But, inside five minutes, his foot became heavy, and the trees began whizzing by. He glanced at Pornsen. The *gapt's* rigid back and set teeth showed that he was again thinking of the report he would make to the chief Uzzite back in the spaceship. He looked furious enough to demand the 'Meter for his ward.

Hal Yarrow breathed deeply of the wind battering his face mask. To H with Pornsen! To H with the 'Meter! The blood lurched in his veins. The air of this planet was not the stuffy air of Earth. His lungs sucked it in like a happy bellows. At that moment, he felt as if he could have snapped his fingers under the nose of the Archurielite himself.

"Look out!" screamed Pornsen.

Hal, out of the corners of his eyes, glimpsed the large antelope-like beast that leaped from the forest onto the road just ahead of the right side of the car. At the same time, he twisted the wheel to swing the vehicle away from it. The vehicle skidded on the dirt.

Its rear swung around. And Hal was not grounded enough in the elements of driving to know that he should turn the wheels in the direction of the skid to straighten the car out.

His lack of knowledge was not fatal, except to the beast, for its bulk struck the vehicle's right side. Its long horns caught in Pornsen's jacket and ripped open the sleeve on his right arm.

The car, its skid checked by the big bulk of the antelope, straightened out. But it was going in a straight line that angled off the road and led it up a sloping ridge of earth. Reaching the end of the ridge, it leaped out into the air and landed with an all-at-once bang of four tires blowing.

Even that impact did not halt it. A big bush loomed before Hal. He jerked on the wheel. Too late.

His chest pushed hard against the wheel as if it were trying to telescope the steering shaft against the dashboard. Fobo slammed into Hal's back, increasing the weight on his chest. Both cried out, and the wog fell away.

Then, except for a hissing, there was silence. A pillar of steam from the broken radiator shot through the branches that held Hal's face in a rough, barky embrace.

Hal Yarrow stared through steamshapes into big brown eyes. He shook his head. Eyes? And arms like branches? Or branches like arms? He thought he was in the grip of a brown-eyed nymph. Or were they called dryads? He couldn't ask anybody. They weren't supposed to know about such creatures. *Nymph* and *dryad* had been deleted from all books including Hack's edition of the *Revised and Real Milton*. Only because Hal was a linguist had he had the chance to read an unexpurgated *Paradise Lost* and thus learn of classical Greek mythology.

Thoughts flashed off and on like lights on a spaceship's control board. Nymphs sometimes turned into trees to escape their pursuers. Was this one of the fabled forest women staring at him with large and beautiful eyes through the longest lashes he'd ever seen?

He shut his eyes and wondered if a head injury was responsible for the vision and, if so, if it would be permanent. Hallucinations like that were worth keeping. He didn't care if they conformed to reality or not.

He opened his eyes. The hallucination was gone.

He thought, *It was that antelope looking at me. It got away after all. It ran around the bush and looked back. Antelope eyes. And my dark self formed the head around the eyes, the long black hair, the slender white neck, the swelling breasts . . . No! Unreal! It was my diseased mind, stunned by the shock, momentarily opened to that which has been festering, seething all that time on the ship without ever seeing a woman, even on the tapes . . .*

He forgot about the eyes. He was choking. A heavy nauseating odor hung over the car. The crash must have frightened the wogs very much. Otherwise, they would not have involuntarily relaxed the sphincter muscles which controlled the neck of the "madbag." This organ, a bladder located near the small of the back, had been used by the presentient ancestors of the Ozagenians as a powerful defensive weapon, much like that of the bombardier beetle. Now an almost vestigial organ, the madbag served as a means of relieving extreme nervous tension. Its function was effective, but its use presented problems. The wog psychiatrists, for instance, either had to keep their windows wide open during therapy or else wear gas masks.

Keoki Amiel Pornsen, assisted by Zugu, crawled out from under the bush into which he had been thrown. His big paunch, the azure color of his uniform, and the white nylon angel's wings sewn on the back of his jacket made him resemble a fat blue bug. He stood up and removed his windmask, showing a bloodless face. His shaking fingers fumbled over the crossed hourglass and sword, symbol of the Haijac Union. Finally, they found the flap for which he was searching. He pulled the magnetic lips of the pocket loose and took out a pack of Merciful Seraphim. Once the cigarette was in his lips, he had a shaky time holding his lighter to it.

Hal held the glowing coil of his own lighter to the tip of Pornsen's cigarette. His hand was steady.

Thirty-one years of discipline shoved back the grin he felt deep inside his face.

Pornsen accepted the light. A second later, a tremor around his lips revealed that he knew he had lost much of his advantage over Yarrow. He realized he couldn't allow a man to do him a service—even one as slight as this—and then crack the whip on him.

Nevertheless, he began formally, "Hal Shamshiel Yarrow . . ."

"*Shib, abba,* I hear and obey," replied Hal as formally.

"Just how do you explain this accident?"

Hal was surprised. Pornsen's voice was much milder than he had expected. He did not relax, however, for he suspected that Pornsen meant to take him off guard and lash out at him when he was not mentally braced for an attack.

"I—or, rather, the Backrunner in me—departed from reality. I—my dark self—willfully precipitated a pseudofuture."

"Oh, really?" said Pornsen, quietly but with a note of sarcasm. "You say your dark self, the Backrunner in you, did that? That is what you have said ever since you were able to talk. Why must you always blame someone else? You know—you should, for I have been forced to whip you many times—that you and you alone are responsible. When you were taught that it was your dark self that caused departures from reality, you were also taught that the Backrunner could cause nothing unless you—your real self, Hal Yarrow—fully cooperated."

"That is as *shib* as the Forerunner's left hand," said Hal. "But, my beloved *gapt,* you forgot one thing in that little lecture of yours."

Now, his voice had a sarcasm to match that in Pornsen's.

Pornsen, shrilly, said, "What do you mean?"

"I mean," said Hal triumphantly, "that you were in the accident, too! Therefore, you caused it just as much as I did!"

Pornsen goggled at him. He said, whining, "But—but, you were driving the car!"

"Makes no difference according to what you have always told me!" said Hal. He was grinning smugly. "You agreed to be in the collision. If you had not, we would have missed the beast."

Pornsen stopped to puff on the cigarette. His hand shook. Yarrow watched the hand that hung free by Pornsen's side, its fingers twisting the seven leather lashes of the whip handle stuck in his belt.

Pornsen said, "You have always shown signs of a regrettable pride and independence. That smacks of behavior that does not conform to the structure of the universe as revealed to mankind by the Forerunner, real be his name.

"I have [puff]—may the Forerunner forgive them! —sent two dozen men and women to II. I did not like to do that, for I loved them with all my heart and self. I wept when I reported them to the holy hierarchy, for I am a tender-hearted man. [Puff!] But it was my duty as a Guardian Angel *Pro Tempore* to watch out for the loathsome diseases of self that may spread and infect the followers of Sigmen. Unreality must not be tolerated. The self is too weak and precious to be subjected to temptation.

"I have been your *gapt* since you were born. [Puff!] You always were a disobedient child. But you could be loved into submissiveness and contrition; you felt my love often. [Puff!]"

Yarrow felt his back tingle. He watched the *gapt's* hand tighten around the handle of the "lover" projecting from the belt.

"However, not until you were eighteen did you really depart from the true future and show your weakness for pseudofutures. That was when you decided to become a *joat* instead of a specialist. I warned you that as a *joat* you'd get only so far in our society. But you persisted. And since we do have need of *joats,* and since I was overruled by my superiors, I allowed you to become one.

"That was [puff] *unshib* enough. But when I picked out the woman most suitable to be your wife—as was my duty and right—for who but your loving *gapt* knows the type of woman best suited for you?—I saw just how proud and unreal you were. You argued and protested and tried to go over my head and held out for a year before you consented to marry her. In that year of unreal behavior, you cost the Sturch one self . . . "

Hal's face paled, revealing seven thin red marks that rayed out from the left corner of his lips and across his cheek to his ear.

"I cost the Sturch nothing!" Hal growled. "Mary and I were married nine years, but we had no children. Tests showed that neither of us was physically sterile. Therefore, one or both was not thinking fertile. I petitioned for a divorce, even though I knew I might end up in H. Why didn't you insist on our divorce, as your duty required, instead of pigeonholing my petition?"

Pornsen blew out smoke nonchalantly enough, but he dropped one shoulder lower than the other as if something had caved inside him. Yarrow, seeing this, knew that he had his *gapt* on the defensive.

Pornsen said, "When I first realized you were on the *Gabriel,* I was sure that you were not on it because of a desire to serve the Sturch. I [puff] thought at the time that you signed up for one reason. And now I am *shib, shib* to the bone, that your reason was your wicked desire to get away from your wife. And, since barrenness, adultery, and interstellar travel are the only legal grounds for divorce, and adultery means going to H, you [puff] took the only way out. You became legally dead by becoming a crewman of the *Gabriel.* You—"

"Don't talk about anything legal to me!" shouted Hal. He shook with rage and, at the same time, hated himself because he could not hide his emotion.

"You know you were not carrying out the proper functions of a *gapt* when you sidetracked my request! I had to sign up—"

"Ah, I thought so!" said Pornsen. He smiled and puffed out smoke and said, "I turned it down because I thought it would be unreal. You see, I had a dream, a very vivid dream, in which I saw Mary bearing your child at the end of two years. It was not a false dream but one that had the unmistakable signs of a revelation sent by the Forerunner. I knew after that dream that your desire for a divorce was a desire for a pseudofuture. I knew that the true future was in my hands and that only by guiding your conduct could I bring it about. I recorded this dream the day after I had it, which was only a week after I reviewed your petition, and—"

"You proved that you were betrayed by a dream sent by the Backrunner and did not see a revelation sent by the Forerunner!" shouted Hal again. "Pornsen, I am going to report this! Out of your own mouth you have convicted yourself!"

Pornsen turned pale; his mouth hung open so the cigarette dropped to the ground; his jowls quivered with fright. "Wha—what do you mean?"

"How could she have my child at the end of two years when I am not on Earth to father it? So, what you *say* you dreamed can't possibly become a real future! Therefore, you allowed yourself to be deceived by the Backrunner. And you know what that means! That you are a candidate for H!"

The *gapt* stiffened. His lower left shoulder drew level with the other. His right hand shot to the handle of the whip, closed around the *crux ansata* on its end, and he pulled it from his belt. It cracked in the air, a few inches from Hal's face.

"See this?" shrieked Pornsen. "Seven lashes! One

for each of the Seven Deadly Unrealities! You've felt them before; you'll feel them again!"

Harshly, Hal said, "Shut up!"

Again, Pornsen's jaw dropped. Whining, he said, "How, how dare you? I, your beloved *gapt*, am—"

"I told you to shut up!" said Hal, less loudly but just as bitingly. "I'm sick of your whine. I've been sick of it for years, my whole life."

Even as he spoke, he watched Fobo walking toward them. Behind Fobo, the antelope lay dead on the road.

The animal is dead, Hal thought. *I thought it had managed to get away. Those eyes staring through the bush at me. Antelope eyes? But if it is dead, whose eyes did I see?*

Pornsen's voice recalled Hal to the present.

"I think, my son, that we spoke in anger, not in premeditated evil. Let us forgive one another, and we'll say nothing to the Uzzites when we get back to the ship."

"*Shib* with me if it's with you," said Hal.

Hal was surprised to see tears welling in Pornsen's eyes. And he was even more surprised, almost shocked, when Pornsen made an attempt to put his arm around Hal's shoulder.

"Ah, my boy, if you only knew how much I loved you, how much it has hurt me when I've had to punish you."

"I find that rather hard to believe," said Hal, and he walked away from Pornsen and toward Fobo.

Fobo, too, had large tears in his unhumanly large and round eyes. But they were from another cause. He was weeping because of sympathy for the beast and shock from the accident. However, with every step toward Hal, his expression became less grieved, and tears dried. He was making a circular sign over himself with his right index finger.

It was, Hal knew, a religious sign which the wogs used in many different situations. Now, Fobo seemed to be using it to relieve his tension. Suddenly, he smiled the ghastly V-in-V smile of a wogglebug. And he was in good spirits. Though supersensitive, his nervous system was hit and run. Charge and discharge came easily.

Fobo stopped before them and said, "A clash of personalities, gentlemen? A disagreement, an argument, a dispute?"

"No," replied Hal. "We were just a little shaken up. Tell me, how far will we have to walk to get to the humanoid ruins? Your car's wrecked. Tell Zugu I'm sorry."

"Do not bother your skulls . . . heads. Zugu was ready to build a new and better vehicle. As for the walk, it will be pleasant and stimulating. It is only a . . . kilometer? Or thereabouts."

Hal threw his mask and goggles into the car, where the Ozagenians had put theirs. He picked up his suitcase from the floor in the compartment back of the rear seat. He left the *gapt's* on the floor. Not without a slight pang of guilt, however, for he knew that as Pornsen's ward, he should have offered to carry it.

"To H with him," he muttered.

He said to Fobo, "Aren't you afraid the driving clothes will be stolen?"

"Pardon?" said Fobo, eager to learn a new word. "Stolen means what?"

"To take an article of property from someone by stealth, without their permission, and keep it for yourself. It is a crime, punishable by law."

"A crime?"

Hal gave up and began walking swiftly up the road. Behind him the *gapt,* angry because he had been rejected and because his ward was breaking etiquette by forcing him to carry his own case, shouted, "Don't presume too far, you—you *joat!*"

Hal didn't turn back but plunged on ahead. The angry retort he had been phrasing beneath his breath fizzed away. Out of the corner of his eye, he had glimpsed white skin in the green foliage.

It was only a flash, gone as quickly as it had come. And he could not be sure that it was not a bird's white wing opening. Yes, he could be. There were no birds on Ozagen.

7

"Soo Yarrow. Soo Yarrow. Wuhfvayfvoo, soo Yarrow."

Hal woke up. For a moment, he had trouble placing himself. Then, as he became wider awake, he recalled that he was sleeping in one of the marble rooms of the ruins. The moonlight, brighter than Earth's, poured in through the doorway. It shone on a small shape clinging upside down to the arch of the doorway. It glittered briefly on a flying insect that passed below the shape. Something long and thin flickered down and caught the flier and pulled it into a suddenly gaping mouth.

The lizard loaned by the ruins custodians was doing a fine job of keeping out pests.

Hal turned his head to look at the open window a foot above him. The bugcatcher there was also busily tonguing the area clean of mosquitoes.

The voice had seemed to come from beyond that moonwashed and narrow rectangle. He strained his ears as if he could force the silence to yield the voice again. But there was only more silence. Then, he jumped and whirled around as a snuffling and rattling came from behind him. A thing the size of a raccoon stood in the doorway. It was one of the quasi-insects, the so-called lungbugs, that prowled the forest at night. It represented a development of arthropod not

71

found on Earth. Unlike its Terran cousins, it did not depend solely on tracheae or breathing tubes for oxygen. A pair of distensible sacs, like a frog's, swelled out and fell in behind its mouth. It was these that had made the snuffling sound.

Though the lungbug was shaped like the sinister praying mantis, Hal didn't worry. Fobo had told him it was not dangerous to a man.

A shrill sound like that of an alarm clock suddenly filled the room. Pornsen sat up on the cot against the wall. Seeing the insect, he yelled. It scurried off. The noise, which had come from the mechanism on Pornsen's wrist, stopped.

Pornsen lay back. He groaned, "That makes the sixth time those *sib* bugs have woke me up."

"Turn off the wristbox," said Hal.

"So you can sneak out of the room and spill your seed on the ground," replied Pornsen.

"You have no right to accuse me of such unreal conduct," said Hal. He spoke mechanically, without deep anger. He was thinking of the voice.

"The Forerunner himself said no one was beyond reproach," muttered Pornsen. He sighed and mumbled as he fell asleep, "Wonder if the rumor is true . . . Forerunner himself may be on this planet . . . watching us . . . he predicted . . . aah . . ."

Hal sat on his cot and watched Pornsen until he began snoring. Hal's own lids felt heavy. Surely, he must have dreamed of that soft, low voice speaking in a tongue neither Terran nor Ozagenian. He must have, because it had been human, and he and the *gapt* were the only specimens of *Homo sapiens* for two hundred miles in any direction.

It had been a woman's voice. Forerunner! To hear a woman again! Not Mary. He never wanted to hear her voice again or even hear *of* her. She was the only woman he had ever—dare he say it to himself?—*had*. That had been a sorry, disgusting, and humiliating ordeal. But it had not taken from him the wish—he was glad that the Forerunner was not there to read his mind—to meet another woman who might give him that ecstasy of which he knew nothing except from spilling his seed—Forerunner help him!—and which was, he was sure, only a paleness and a hollowness compared to that which waited . . .

"*Soo Yarrow. Wuhfvayfvoo. Sa mfa, zh'net Tastinak. R'gateh wa f'net.*"

Slowly, Hal rose from the cot. His neck was cased in ice. The whisper *was* coming from the window. He looked at it. The outline of a woman's head tilted into the solid box of moonlight that was window. The solid box became a cascade. Moonwash flowed over white shoulders. The white of a finger crossed the black of a mouth.

"*Poo wamoo tu baw choo. E'ooteh. Seelahs. Fvooneh. Fvit, seelfvoopleh.*"

Numbed, but obeying as if shot full of hypno-lipno, he began walking toward the doorway. He was not so shocked, however, that he did not look at Pornsen to make sure he was still sleeping.

For a second, his reflexes almost overcame him and forced him to wake up the *gapt*. But he withdrew the hand reaching for Pornsen. He must take a chance. The urgency and fear in the woman's voice told him that she was desperate and needed him. And it was evident that she did not want him to arouse Pornsen.

What would Pornsen say, do, if he knew there was a woman outside this very room?

Woman? How could a woman be here?

Her words had clicked something familiar. He had had the strange and fleeting notion that he should know the language. But he did not.

He stopped. What was he thinking of? If Pornsen woke and looked over at the cot to make sure his ward was still in it . . . He went back to the cot and shoved his suitcase under the sheet which the custodian had provided for him. He rolled up his jacket and packed it next to the case. One end of it stuck out of the sheet and lay on the pillow. Perhaps, if Pornsen was very sleepy, he might mistake the dark lump on the pillow and the bulk under the sheet for Hal.

Softly, on bare feet, he walked again toward the doorway. An object about eight decimeters high stood on guard in it. A statuette of the archangel Gabriel, pale, wings half-extended, a sword in its right hand held above its head.

If any object with a mass larger than a mouse's came within two feet of the field radiating from the statuette, it would cause a signal to be transmitted to the small case mounted on the silver bracelet around Pornsen's wrist. The case would shrill—as it had at the appearance of the lungbug—and up would come Pornsen from the bottom of his sleep.

The statuette's purpose was not only to insure against trespassers. It was also there to make certain that Hal would not leave the room without his *gapt's* knowledge. As the ruins had no working plumbing, Hal's only excuse to step outside would be to relieve himself. The *gapt* would go along to see that he did not try to do something else.

Hal picked up a fly swatter. It had a three-foot-long handle made of some flexible wood. Its mass would not be enough to touch off the field. Hand trembling, he very gently pushed the statuette to one side with the end of the handle. He had to be careful not to upset it, for tilting triggered its alarm. Fortunately, the stone floor was one of those which had had the debris, piled on by centuries, cleaned out. The stone beneath was smooth, polished by generations of feet.

Once outside, Hal reached back in and slid the object back to its former spot. Then, with his heart pounding under the double strain of tampering with the statuette and of meeting a strange woman, he walked around the corner.

The woman had moved from the window into the shadow of a statue of a kneeling goddess about forty yards away. He began walking toward her, then he saw why she was hiding. Fobo was strolling toward him. Hal walked faster. He wanted to intercept the wog before he noticed the girl and also before Fobo was so close that their voices might waken Pornsen.

"Shalom, aloha, good dreaming, Sigmen love you," said Fobo. "You seem nervous. Is it that incident of the forenoon?"

"No. I am just restless. And I wanted to admire these ruins by moonlight."

"Grand, beautiful, weird, and a little sad," said Fobo. "I think of these people, of the many generations that lived here, how they were born, played, laughed, wept, suffered, gave birth, and died. And all, all, every one dead and turned to dust. Ah, Hal, it brings tears to my eyes and a premonition of my own doom."

Fobo pulled a handkerchief from the pouch on his belt and blew his nose.

Hal looked at Fobo. How human—in some respects —was this monster, this native of Ozagen. Ozagen. A strange name with a story. What was the story? That the discoverer of this planet, upon first seeing the natives, had exclaimed, "Oz again!"

It was only natural. The aborigines resembled Frank Baum's Professor Wogglebug. Their bodies were rather round, and their limbs were skinny in proportion. Their mouths were shaped like two broad and shallow V's, one set inside the other. The lips were thick and lobular. Actually, a wogglebug had four lips, each leg of the two V's being separated by a deep seam at the connection. Once, far back on the evolutionary path, those lips had been modified arms. Now they were rudimentary limbs, so disguised as true labial parts and so functional that no one could have guessed their origin. When the wide V-in-V mouths opened in a laugh, they startled the Terrans. They had no teeth but serrated ridges of jawbone. A fold of skin hung from the roof of the mouth. Once the epipharynx, it was now a vestigial upper tongue. It was this organ which gave the underlying trill to so many Ozagen sounds and gave the human beings so much trouble reproducing them.

Their skins were as lightly pigmented as Hal's, and he was a redhead. But where his was pink, theirs was a very faint green. Copper, not iron, carried oxygen in their blood cells. Or so they said. So far they had refused to allow the Haijac to take blood samples. But they had promised that they might give permission within the next four or five weeks. Their reluctance, so they had stated, was caused by certain religious taboos. If, however, they could be assured that the Earthmen would not be drinking the blood, they might let them have it.

Macneff thought they were lying, but he had no good reasons for this. It was impossible for the Ozagenians to know just why their blood was wanted.

That their blood cells used copper instead of iron should have made the Ozagenians considerably less strong and less enduring in physical exertion than the Terrans. Their corpuscles would not transport oxygen as efficiently. But Nature had made certain compensations. Fobo had two hearts, which beat faster than Hal's and drove blood through arteries and veins larger than Hal's.

Nevertheless, the fastest sprinter or marathon runner of this planet would be left behind by his Terrestrial counterpart.

Hal had borrowed a book on evolution. But, since he could read very little of it, he had so far had to content himself with looking at the many illustrations. The wog, however, had explained what they represented.

Hal had refused to believe Fobo.

"You say that mammalian life originated from a primeval sea worm! That has to be wrong! We know that the first land lifeform was an amphibian. Its fins developed into legs; it lost its ability to get oxygen from sea water. It evolved into a reptile, then a primitive mammal, then an insectivorous creature, then a

presimian, then a simian, and eventually into the sa-
pient bipedal stage, and then into modern man!"

"Is that so?" Fobo had said calmly. "I don't doubt
that things went just as you said. On Earth. But here
evolution took a different course. Here there were
three ancestral *se"ba'takufu,* that is, *motherworms.*
One had hemoglobin-bearing blood cells; one, copper-
bearing; one, vanadium-bearing. The first had a natural advantage over the other two, but for some reason
it dominated this continent but not the other. We have
some evidence that the first also split early into two
lines, both of which were notochords but one of which
wasn't mammalian.

"Anyway, all the motherworms did have fins, and
these evolved into limbs. And—"

"But," Hal had said, "evolution can't work that
way! Your scientists have made a serious, a grievous,
error. After all, your paleontology is just beginning;
it's only about a hundred years old."

"Ah!" Fobo had said. "You're too terrocentric.
Hidebound. You have an anemic imagination. Your
thought arteries are hardened. Consider the possibility that there might be billions of habitable planets in
this universe and that on each evolution may have
taken slightly, or even vastly, different paths. The
Great Goddess is an experimenter. She'd get bored
reproducing the same thing over and over. Wouldn't
you?"

Hal was sure that the wogs were mistaken. Unfortunately, they weren't going to live long enough to be
illuminated by the superior and much older science of
the Haijac.

Now Fobo had removed his skullcap with its two
imitation antennae, the symbols of the Grasshopper
clan. But, even though this removal lessened his resemblance to Professor Wogglebug, his bald forepate
and the stiff blond corkscrew fuzz on his backpate re-
asserted it. And the bridgeless, comically long nose
shooting straight out from his face doubly strengthened

it. Concealed in its cartilaginous length were two antennae, his organs of smell.

The Terran who first saw the Ozagenians would have been justified in his remark, if he had made it. But it was doubtful if he had. In the first place, the local tongue used the word *Ozagen* for Mother Earth. In the second place, even if the man on the first expedition had thought this, he would not have uttered it. The Oz books were forbidden in the Haijac Union; he could not have read the term unless he had taken a chance on buying it from a booklegger. It was possible he had. In fact, that was the only explanation. Otherwise, how could the spaceman who told Hal the story have come by the word? The originator of the story may not have cared if the authorities found out he was reading condemned books. Spacemen were famous, or infamous, for their disregard of danger and lax conduct in following the precepts of the Sturch when not on Earth.

Hal became aware that Fobo was talking to him.

". . . this *joat* that Monsieur Pornsen called you when he was so angry and furious. What does that mean?"

"It means," he said, "'a person who is not a specialist in any of the sciences but who knows much about all of them. Actually, I am a liaison officer between various scientists and government officials. It is my business to summarize and integrate current scientific reports and then present them to the hierarchy."

He glanced at the statue.

The woman was not in sight.

"Science," he continued, "has become so specialized that intelligible communication even among scientists in the same field is very difficult. Each scientist has a deep vertical knowledge of his own little area but not much horizontal knowledge. The more he knows about his own subject, the less aware he is of what others in allied subjects are doing. He just does not have the time to read even a fraction of the overwhelming mass of articles. It is so bad that of two doctors who specialize in nose dysfunctions, one will treat the left nostril and the other will treat the right."

Fobo threw up his hands in horror.

"But science would come to a standstill! Surely you exaggerate!"

"About doctors, yes," said Hal, managing to grin a little. "But I do not exaggerate much. And it is true that science is not advancing in geometric progression as it once did. There is a lack of time for the scientist and too little communication. He cannot be aided in his own research by a discovery in another field because he just will not hear of it."

Hal saw a head stick out from the base of the statue and then withdraw. He began to sweat.

Fobo questioned Hal about the religion of the Forerunner. Hal was as taciturn as possible and completely ignored some questions, though he felt embarrassed by doing so. The wog was nothing if not logical, and logic was a light that Hal had never turned upon what he had been taught by the Urielites.

Finally, he said, "All I can say to you is that it is absolutely true that most men can travel subjectively in time but that the Forerunner, his evil disciple, the Backrunner, and the Backrunner's wife are the only people who can travel objectively in time. I know it is true because the Forerunner predicted what would happen in the future, and his every prediction was fulfilled. And—"

"Every prediction?"

"Well, all but one. But that turned out to be an unreal forecast, a pseudofuture somehow inserted by the Backrunner into *The Western Talmud*."

"How do you know those predictions which haven't been fulfilled aren't also false insertions?"

"Well . . . we don't. The only way to tell is to wait until the time for them to happen arrives. Then . . ."

Fobo smiled and said, "Then you know that that particular prediction was written and inserted by the Backrunner."

"Of course. But the Urielites have been working for

some years now on a method which they say will prove, by internal evidence, whether the future events are real futures or false. When we left Earth, we expected to hear at any time that an infallible method had been discovered. Now, of course, we won't know until we return to Earth."

"I feel that this conversation is making you nervous," said Fobo. "Perhaps, we can pursue it some other time. Tell me, what do you think of the ruins?"

"Very interesting. Of course, I take an almost personal interest in this vanished people because they were mammals, so much like us Terrans. What I cannot imagine is how they could almost die out. If they were like us, and they seem to have been, they would have thrived."

"They were a very decadent, quarrelsome, greedy, bloody, pernicious breed," Fobo said. "Though, no doubt, there were many fine people among them. I doubt that they all killed each other off, except for a few dozen or so. I doubt also that a plague killed almost all their kind. Maybe someday we'll find out. Right now, I'm tired, so I'm going to bed."

"I'm restless. If you don't mind, I'll poke around. These ruins are so beautiful in this bright moonlight."

"Reminds me of a poem by our great bard Shamero. If I could remember it and could translate it effectively enough into American, I'd recite it to you."

Fobo's V-in-V lips yawned.

"I shall go to bed, retire, wrap the arms of Morpheus around me. However, first, do you have any weapons, firearms, with which to defend yourself against the things that prowl the night?"

"I am allowed to carry a knife in my bootsheath," said Hal.

Fobo reached under his cloak and brought out a pistol. He handed it to Hal and said, "Here! I hope you won't have to use it, but you never know. We live in a savage, predatory world, my friend. Especially out here in the country."

Hal looked curiously at the weapon, similar to those he had seen in Siddo. It was crude compared to the small automatics in the *Gabriel,* but it had all the aura and fascination of an alien weapon. Plus the fact that it resembled very much the early steel pistols of Earth. Its hexagonal barrel was not quite three decimeters long; the caliber looked to be about ten millimeters. A revolving chamber contained five brass cartridges; these were loaded with black gunpowder, lead bullets, and percussion caps containing, he guessed, fulminate of mercury. Strangely, the pistol had no trigger; a strong spring pulled the hammer down against the cartridge when the finger released the hammer.

Hal would have liked to see the mechanism that turned the revolving cartridge chamber when the hammer was pulled back. But he did not want to keep Fobo around any longer than he could help.

Nevertheless, he could not refrain from asking him why the Siddo did not use a trigger. Fobo was surprised at the question. When he had heard Hal's explanation, he blinked his large round eyes (a weird and at first unnerving sight because the lower eyelid made the motion), and he said, "I have never thought of it! It does seem to be more efficient and less tiring on the handler of the gun, does it not?"

"Obvious to me," said Hal. "But then, I am an Earthman and think like one. I have noticed the not unsurprising fact that you Ozagens do not always think as we do."

He handed the gun back to Fobo, and he said, "I am sorry I can't take it. But I am forbidden to carry firearms."

Fobo looked puzzled, but evidently he did not think it politic to inquire why not. Or else he was too tired.

He said, "Very well. Shalom, aloha, good dreaming, Sigmen visit you."

"Shalom to you, too," said Hal. He watched the broad back of the wog disappear into the shadows, and he felt a strange warmth for the creature. Despite his utterly alien and unhuman appearance, Fobo appealed to Hal.

Hal turned and walked toward the statue of the Great Mother. When he got to the shadows at its base, he saw the woman slipping into the darkness cast by a three-story heap of rubble. He followed her to the rubble only to see her several stone-throws ahead, leaning against a monolith. Beyond was the lake, silvery and black in the moonlight.

Hal walked toward her and was about five meters from her when she spoke in a low and throaty voice.

"Baw sfa, soo Yarrow."

"Baw sfa," he echoed, knowing that it must be a greeting in her language.

"Baw sfa," she repeated, and then, obviously translating the phrase for his benefit, she said, in Siddo, *" 'Abhu'umaigeitsi'i."*

Which meant, very roughly, "Good evening."

He gasped.

8

OF course! Now he knew why the words had sounded vaguely familiar and the rhythm of her speech reminded him so strongly of a not too unrecent experience. Something about it stirred up a memory of his research in the tiny community of the last of the French speakers in the Hudson Bay Preserve.

Baw sfa. Baw sfa was *bon soir*.

Even though her speech was, linguistically speaking, a very decayed form, it could not disguise its ancestry. *Baw sfa*. And those other words he had heard through the window. *Wuhfvayfvoo*. That would be *levez-vous*, French for "get up."

Soo Yarrow. Could that be, must be, *Monsieur* Yarrow? The initial *m* dropped, the French *eu* evolved to something resembling the American *u* sound? Must be. And there were other changes to this degenerate French. Development of aspiration. The abandonment of nasalization. Vowel shift. Replacement of *k* before a vowel by a glottal stop. Change of *d* to *t; l* to *w; f* shifted to a sound between *v* and *f; w* changed to *f*. What else? There must also be a transmutation in the meanings of some words, and new words replacing old ones.

Yet, despite its unfamiliarity, it was subtly Gallic. "*Baw sfa*," he repeated.

And he thought, How inadequate that greeting!

Here were two human beings meeting forty-odd light-years from Earth, a man who had not seen a woman for one subjective year, a woman obviously hiding and in great fear, perhaps the only woman left on this planet. And he could only say, "Good evening."

He stepped closer. And he flushed with the heat of embarrassment. Almost, he turned and ran. Her white skin was relieved only by two black narrow strips of cloth, one across her breasts, the other diapered around the hips. It was a sight such as he had never seen in his life except in a forbidden photograph.

The embarrassment was forgotten almost at once as he saw that she was wearing lipstick. He gasped and felt a shock of fear. Her lips were as scarlet as those of the monstrously evil wife of the Backrunner.

He forced himself to quit shaking. He must think rationally. This woman could not be Anna Changer, come from the far distant past to this planet to seduce him, to turn him against the real religion. She would not speak this degraded French if she were Anna Changer. Nor would she appear to as insignificant a person as Hal. She would have come to the chief Urielite, Macneff.

His mind gave the problem of the lipstick a quick flip and considered its other side. Cosmetics had gone out with the coming of the Forerunner. No woman dared . . . well, that wasn't true . . . it was just in the Haijac Union that cosmetics were not used. Israeli, Malay, and Bantu women wore rouge. But then everybody knew what kind of women they were.

Another step, and he was close enough to determine that the scarlet was natural, not paint. He felt an immense relief. She could not be the wife of the Backrunner. She could not even be Earthborn. She had to be an Ozagen humanoid. The murals on the walls of the ruins depicted red-lipped women, and Fobo had told him that these had been born with the flaming labile pigment.

The answer to one question bore another. Why was she speaking a Terran language, or, rather, a descendant of one? This tongue, he was sure, did not exist on Earth.

The next moment, he forgot his questions. She was clinging to him, and he had his arms around her, clumsily trying to comfort her. She was weeping and pouring out words, one so fast after the other that even though he knew they came from the French he could only make out a word here and there.

Hal asked her to slow down and to go over what she had said. She paused, her head cocked slightly to the left, then brushed back her hair. It was a gesture he was to find characteristic of her when she was thinking.

She began to repeat very slowly. But, as she continued, she speeded up, her full lips working like two bright red creatures independent of her, packed with their own life and purpose.

Fascinated, Hal watched them.

Ashamed, he looked away from them, tried to look into her wide dark eyes, could not meet them, and looked to one side of her head.

She told her story disconnectedly and with much repetition and backtracking. Many of her words he could not understand but had to supply the meaning from the context. But he could understand that her name was Jeannette Rastignac. That she came from a plateau in the central mountains of this continent. That she and her three sisters were, as far as she knew, the only survivors of her kind. That she had been captured by an exploring party of wogs who'd intended to take her to Siddo. That she had escaped and had been hiding in the ruins and in the surrounding forest. That she was frightened because of the terrible things that prowled the forest at night. That she lived on wild fruit and berries or on food stolen from wog farmhouses. That she had seen Hal when his vehicle hit the antelope. Yes, it had been her eyes he had thought were those of the antelope.

"How did you know my name?" Hal said.

"I followed you and listened to you talk. I could not

understand you. But, after a while, I heard you respond to the name of Hal Yarrow. Learning your name was nothing at all. What puzzled me was that you and that other man looked like my father, must be human beings. Yet, because you did not speak my father's language, you could not have come from his planet.

"Then, I thought, of course! My father had once told me that his people had come to *Wuhbopfey* from another planet. So, it was a matter of logic. You must be from there, the original world of human beings."

"I don't understand at all," said Hal. "Your father's ancestors came to this planet, Ozagen? But . . . but there is no record of that! Fobo told me—"

"No, no, you do not understand, yes! My father, Jean-Jacques Rastignac, was born on another planet. He came to this one from that. His ancestors came to that other planet which revolves around a star far from here from an even more distant star."

"Oh, then they must have been colonists from Earth. But there is no record of that. At least, none that I have ever seen. They must have been French. But if that is true, they left Earth and went to that other system over two hundred years ago. And they could not have been Canadian French, for there were too few of them left after the Apocalyptic War. They must have been European French. But the last speaker of French in Europe died two and a half centuries ago. So—"

"It is confusing, *nespfa?* All I know is what my father told me. He said he and some others from *Wuhbopfey* found Ozagen during an exploration. They landed on this continent, his comrades were killed, he found my mother—"

"Your mother? Worse and worse," Hal said, groaning.

"She was an indigene. Her people have always been here. They built this city. They—"

"And your father was an Earthman? And you were born of his union with an Ozagen humanoid? Impossible! The chromosomes of your father and of your mother could not possibly have matched!"

"I do not care about these chromosomes!" said Jeannette in a quavering voice. "You see me before you, do you not? I exist, do I not? My father lay with my mother, and here I am. Deny me if you can."

"I did not mean . . . I mean . . . it seemed . . ." He stopped and looked at her, not knowing what to say.

Suddenly, she began sobbing. She tightened her arms around him, and his hands pressed down on her shoulders. They were soft and smooth, and her breasts pressed against his ribs.

"Save me," she said brokenly. "I cannot stand this any more. You must take me with you. You must save me."

Yarrow thought swiftly. He had to get back to the room in the ruins before Pornsen woke up. And he couldn't see her tomorrow, because a gig from the ship was picking up the two Haijacs in the morning. Whatever he was going to do would have to be unfolded to her in the next few minutes.

Suddenly, he had a plan; it germinated from another idea, one he had long carried around buried in his brain. Its seeds had been in him even before the ship had left Earth. But he hadn't had the courage to carry it out. Now, this girl had appeared, and she was what he needed to spark his guts, make him step onto a path that could not be retraced.

"Jeannette," he said fiercely, "listen to me! You'll have to wait here every night. No matter what things haunt the dark, you'll have to be here. I can't tell you just when I'll be able to get a gig and fly here. Sometime in the next three weeks, I think. If I'm not here by then, keep waiting. *Keep waiting!* I'll be here! And when I am, we'll be safe. Safe for a while, at least. Can you do that? Can you hide here? And wait?"

She nodded her head and said, *"Fi."*

9

TWO weeks later, Yarrow flew from the spaceship *Gabriel* to the ruins. His needle-shaped gig gleamed in the big moon as it floated over the white marble building and settled to a stop. The city lay silent and bleached, great stone cubes and hexagons and cylinders and pyramids and statues like toys left scattered by a giant child who has gone to bed to sleep forever.

Hal stepped out, glanced to his left and right, and then strode to an enormous arch. His flashlight probed its darkness; his voice echoed from the faraway roof and walls.

"Jeannette! Sah mfa. Fo tami, Hal Yarrow. *Jeannette! Ou eh tu?* It's me. Your friend. Where are you?"

He walked down the fifty-meter-broad staircase that led to the crypts of the kings. The beam bounced up and down the steps and suddenly splashed against the black and white figure of the girl.

"Hal!" she cried, looking up at him. "Thank the Great Stone Mother! I've waited every night! But I knew you'd come!"

Tears trembled on the long lashes; her scarlet mouth was trembling as if she were doing her best to keep from sobbing. He wanted to take her in his arms and comfort her, but it was a terrible thing even to look at an unclothed woman. To embrace her would be unthinkable. Nevertheless, that was what he was thinking.

The next minute, as if divining the cause of his paralysis, she moved to him and put her head on his chest. Her own shoulders hunched forward as she tried to burrow into him. He found his arms going around her. His muscles tightened, and blood lunged down into his loins.

He released her and looked away. "We'll talk later. We've no time to lose. Come."

Silently, she followed him until they came to the gig. Then, she hesitated by the door. He gestured impatiently for her to climb in and sit down beside him.

"You will think I'm a coward," she said. "But I have never been in a flying machine. To leave this earth . . ."

Surprised, he could only stare at her.

It was hard for him to understand the attitude of a person totally unaccustomed to air travel.

"Get in!" he barked.

Obediently enough, she got in and sat down in the copilot's seat. She could not keep from trembling, however, or looking with huge brown eyes at the instruments before and around her.

Hal glanced at his watchphone.

"Ten minutes to get to my apartment in the city. One minute to drop you off there. A half-minute to return to the ship. Fifteen minutes to report on my espionage among the wogs. Thirty seconds to return to the apartment. Not quite half an hour in all. Not bad."

He laughed. "I would have been here two days ago, but I had to wait until all the gigs that were on automatic were in use. Then, I pretended that I was in a hurry, that I had forgotten some notes, and that I had to go back to my apartment to pick them up. So, I borrowed one of the manually controlled gigs used for exploration outside the city. I never could have gotten permission from the O.D. for that if he had not been overwhelmed by this."

Hal touched a large golden badge on his left chest. It bore a Hebrew *L*.

"That means I'm one of the Chosen. I've passed the 'Meter."

Jeannette, who had seemingly forgotten her terror, had been looking at Hal's face in the glow from the panel light.

She gave a little cry. "Hal Yarrow! What have they done to you?" Her fingers touched his face.

A deep purple ringed his eyes; his cheeks were sunken, and in one a muscle twitched; a rash spread over his forehead; the seven whipmarks stood out against a pale skin.

"Anybody would say I was crazy to do it," he said. "I stuck my head in the lion's mouth. And he didn't bite my head off. Instead, I bit his tongue."

"What do you mean?"

"Listen. Didn't you think it was strange that Pornsen wasn't with me tonight, breathing his sanctimonious breath down my neck? No? Well, you don't know us. There was only one way I could get permission to move out of my quarters in the ship and get an apartment in Siddo. That is, without having a *gapt* living with me to watch my every move. And without having to leave you out here in the forest. And I couldn't do *that*."

She ran her finger down the line from his nose to the corner of his lip. Ordinarily he would have shrunk from the touch because he hated close contact with anybody. Now, he didn't move back.

"Hal," she said softly. *"Maw sheh."*

He felt a glow. *My dear.* Well, why not?

To stave off the headiness her touch gave, he said, "There was only one thing to do. Volunteer for the 'Meter."

"Wuh Met? 'Es'ase'asah?"

"It's the only thing that can free you from the constant shadow of a *gapt*. Once you've passed it, you're pure, above suspicion—theoretically, at least.

"My petition caught the hierarchy off guard.

They never expected any of the scientists—let alone me—to volunteer. Urielites and Uzzites have to take it if they hope to advance to the hierarchy—"

"Urielites? Uzzites?"

"To put it in ancient terminology, priests and cops. The Forerunner adopted those terms—the names of angels—for religious-governmental use—from the Talmud. See?"

"No."

"I'll explain that later. Anyway, only the most zealous ask to face the 'Meter. It's true that many people do, but only because they are compelled to. The Urielites were gloomy about my chances, but they were forced by law to let me try. Besides, they were bored, and they wanted to be entertained—in their grim fashion."

He scowled at the memory. "A day later, I was told to report to the psych lab at twenty-three hundred S.T.—Ship's Time, that is. I went into my cabin— Pornsen was out—opened my labcase, and took out a bottle labeled 'Prophetsfood.' It is supposed to contain a powder whose base is peyote. That's a drug that was once used by American Indian medicine men."

"Kfe?"

"Just listen. You'll get the main points. Prophetsfood is taken by everybody during Purification Period. That's two days of locking yourself in a cell, fasting, praying, being flagellated by electric whips, and seeing visions induced by hunger and Prophetsfood. Also subjective time-traveling."

"Kfe?"

"Don't keep saying 'What?' I haven't got time to explain dunnology. It took me ten years of hard study to understand it and its mathematics. Even then, there were a lot of questions I had. But I didn't ask them. I might be thought to be doubting.

"Anyway, my bottle did not hold Prophetsfood. Instead, it contained a substitute I'd secretly prepared just before the ship left Earth. That powder was the reason why I dared face the 'Meter. And why I was not as terrified as I should have been . . . though I was scared enough. Believe me."

"I do believe you. You were brave. You overcame your fear."

He felt his face reddening. It was the first time in his life he had ever been complimented.

"A month before the expedition took off for Ozagen, I had noticed, in one of the many scientific journals that I must review, an announcement that a certain drug had been synthesized. Its efficacy was in destroying the virus of the so-called Martian rash. What interested me was a footnote. It was in small print and in Hebrew, which showed that the biochemist must have realized its importance."

"Pookfe?"

"Why? Well, I imagine it was in Hebrew in order to keep any laymen from understanding it. If a secret like that became generally known . . .

"The note commented briefly that it had been found that a man suffering from the rash was temporarily immune to the effects of hypno-lipno. And that the Urielites should take care during any sessions with the 'Meter that their subject was healthy."

"I have trouble understanding you," she said.

"I'll go slower. Hypno-lipno is the most widely used so-called truth-drug. I saw at once the implications in the note. The beginning of the article described how the Martian rash was narcotically induced for experimental purposes. The drug used was not named, but it did not take me long to look it and its processing up in other journals. I thought if the true rash would make a man immune to hypno-lipno, why wouldn't the artificial?

"No sooner said than done. I prepared a batch, inserted a tape of questions about my personal life in a psychotester, injected the rash drug, injected the truthdrug, and swore that I would lie to the tester about my life. And I *could* lie, even though shot full of hypnolipno!"

"You're so clever to think of that," she murmured.

She squeezed his biceps. He hardened them. It was a vain thing to do, but he wanted her to think he was strong.

"Nonsense!" he said. "A blind man would have seen what to do. In fact, I wouldn't be surprised if the Uzzites had arrested the chemist and put out orders for some other truth-drug to be used. If they did, they were too late. Our ship left before any such news reached us.

"Anyway, the first day with the 'Meter was nothing to worry about. I took a twelve-hour written and oral test in serialism. That's Dunne's theories of time and Sigmen's amplifications on it. I've been taking that same test for years. Easy but tiring.

"The next day I rose early, bathed, and ate what was supposed to be Prophetsfood. Breakfastless, I went into the Purification Cell. Alone, I lay two days on a cot. From time to time I took a drink of water or a shot of the false drug. Now and then, I pressed the button that sent the mechanical scourge lashing against me. The more flagellations, you know, the higher your credit.

"I didn't see any visions. I did break out with the rash. That didn't worry me. If anybody got suspicious, I could explain that I had an allergy to Prophetsfood. Some people do."

He looked below. Moon-frosted forest and an occasional square or hexagonal light from a farmhouse. Ahead was the high range of hills that shielded Siddo.

"So," he continued, unconsciously talking faster as the hills loomed closer, "at the end of my purification I rose, dressed, and ate the ceremonial dinner of locusts and honey."

"Ugh!"

"Locusts aren't so bad if you've been eating them since childhood."

"Locusts are delicious," she said. "I've eaten them many times. It's the combination with honey that sickens me."

He shrugged and said, "I'm going to turn out the

cabin lights. Get down on the floor. And put on that cloak and nightmask. You can pass for a wog."

Obediently she slid off the seat. Before he flicked the lights off, he glanced down. She was leaning over while picking up the cloak, and he could not help getting a full glimpse of her superb breasts. Her nipples were as scarlet as her lips. Though he jerked his head away, he kept the image in his head. He felt deeply aroused. The shame, he knew even then, would come later.

He continued uncomfortably: "Then the hierarch came in. Macneff the Sandalphon. After him, the theologians and the dunnological specialists: the psychoneural parallelists, the interventionists, the substratumists, the chronentropists, the pseudotemporalists, the cosmobserverists.

"They sat me down in a chair that was the focus of a modulating magnetic-detector field. They injected hypno-lipno into my arm. They turned out the lights. They said prayers for me, and they chanted chapters from *The Western Talmud* and the *Revised Scriptures*. Then a spotlight was directed upon the Elohimeter—"

" 'Es'ase'asah?"

"*Elohim* is Hebrew for 'God.' A meter is, well, those." He pointed at the instrument panel. "The Elohimeter is round and enormous, and its needle, as long as my arm, is straight up and down. The circumference of the dial's face is marked with Hebraic letters that are supposed to mean something to those giving the test.

"Most people are ignorant of what the needle indicates. But I'm a *joat*. I've access to the books that describe the test."

"Then you knew the answers, *nespfa?*"

"*Fi*. Though that means nothing, because hypno-lipno brings out the truth, the reality . . . unless, of course, you are suffering from Martian rash, natural or artificial."

His sudden laugh was a mirthless bark.

"Under the drug, Jeannette, all the dirty and foul

things you've done and thought, all the hates you've had for your superiors, all the doubts about the realness of the Forerunner's doctrines—these rise up from your lower-level minds like soap released at the bottom of a dirty bathtub. Up it comes, slick and irresistibly buoyant and covered with layers of scum.

"But I sat there, and I watched the needle. It's just like watching the face of God, Jeannette—you can't undersand that, can you?—and I lied. Oh, I didn't overplay it. I didn't pretend to be incredibly pure and faithful. I confessed to minor unrealities. Then the needle would flicker and go back around the circumference a few square letters. But, on the big issues, I answered as if my life depended on them. Which it did.

"And I told them my dreams—my subjective time-traveling."

"Soopji'tiw?"

"Fi. Everybody travels in time subjectively. But the Forerunner is the only man, except for his first disciple and his wife and a few of the scriptural prophets, who has traveled objectively.

"Anyway, my dreams were beauties—architecturally speaking. Just what they liked to hear. My last, and crowning, creation—or lie—was one in which the Forerunner himself appeared on Ozàgen and spoke to the Sandalphon, Macneff. That event is supposed to take place a year from now."

"Oh, Hal," she breathed. "Why did you tell them that?"

"Because now, *maw sheh,* the expedition will not leave Ozagen until that year is up. They couldn't go without giving up the chance of seeing Sigmen in the flesh as he voyages up and down the stream of time. Not without making a liar of him. And of me. So, you see, that colossal lie will make sure that we have at least a year together."

"And then?"

"We'll think of something else then."

Her throaty voice murmured in the darkness by the seat, "And you would do all that for me . . ."

Hal did not reply. He was too busy keeping the gig close to the rooftop level. Clumps of buildings, widely separated by woods, flashed by. So fast was he going that he almost overshot Fobo's castlelike house. Three stories high, medieval in appearance with its crenellated towers and gargoyle heads of stone beasts and insects leering out from many niches, it was no closer than a hundred yards to any other building. Wogs built cities with plenty of elbow room.

Jeannette put on the long-snouted nightmask; the gig's door swung open; they ran across the sidewalk and into the building. After they dashed through the lobby and up the steps to the second floor, they had to stop while Hal fumbled for the key. He had had a wog smith make the lock and a wog carpenter install it. He hadn't trusted the carpenter's mate from the ship because there was too much chance of duplicate keys being made.

He finally found the key but had trouble inserting it. He was breathing hard by the time he succeeded in opening the door. He almost pushed Jeannette through. She had taken her mask off.

"Wait, Hal," she said, leaning her weight against his. "Haven't you forgotten something?"

"Oh, Forerunner! What could it be? Something serious?"

"No. I only thought," and she smiled and then lowered her lids, "that it was the Terran custom for men to carry their brides across the threshold. That is what my father told me."

His jaw dropped. Bride! She was certainly taking a lot for granted!

He couldn't take time to argue. Without a word, he swept her up in his arms and carried her into the apartment. There he put her down and said, "Back as soon as possible. If anybody knocks or tries to get in, hide in that special chamber I had the wog car-

penter build for you inside our closet. Don't make a
sound or come out until you're sure it's me."

She suddenly put her arms around him and kissed
him.

"Maw sheh, maw gwah, maw fooh."

Things were going too fast. He didn't say a word or
even return her kiss. Vaguely he felt that her words,
applied to him, were somewhat ridiculous. If he translated her degenerate French correctly, she had called
him her dear, her big strong man.

Turning, he closed the door but not so quickly that
he did not see the hall light shine on a white face
haloed blackly by a hood. A red mouth stained the
whiteness.

He shook. He had a feeling that Jeannette was not
going to be the frigid mate so much admired, officially,
by the Sturch.

10 𐤊

HAL was an hour late returning home from the *Gabriel* because the Sandalphon asked for more details about the prophecy he had made concerning Sigmen. Then, Hal had to dictate his report on the day's espionage. Afterward, he ordered a sailor to pilot his gig back to the apartment. While he was walking toward the launching rack, he met Pornsen.

"Shalom, *abba*," Hal said.

He smiled and rubbed his knuckles against the raised *lamedh* on the shield.

The *gapt's* left shoulder, always low, sagged even more, as if it were a flag dipping in surrender. If there were any whip cuts to be given, they would be struck by Yarrow.

Hal puffed out his chest and started to walk on, but Pornsen said, "Just a minute, son. Are you going back to the city?"

"*Shib.*"

"*Shib*. I'll ride back with you. I have an apartment in the same building. On the third floor, right opposite Fobo's."

Hal opened his mouth to protest, then closed it. It was Pornsen's turn to smile. He turned and led the way. Hal followed with tight lips. Had the *gapt* trailed him and seen his meeting with Jeanette? No. If he had, he would have had Hal arrested at once.

The *gapt* had one distinguishing feature: a small mind. He knew his presence would annoy Hal and that living in the same building with him would poison Hal's joy at being free from surveillance.

Under his breath Hal quoted an old proverb: "A *gapt's* teeth never let loose."

The sailor was waiting by the gig. They all got in and dropped silently into the night.

At the apartment building, Hal strode into the doorway ahead of Pornsen. He felt a slight glow of satisfaction at thus breaking etiquette and expressing his contempt for the man.

Before opening his door, he paused. The guardian angel passed silently behind him. Hal, struck with a devilish thought, called out, *"Abba."*

Pornsen turned.

"What?"

"Would you care to inspect my rooms and see if I'm hiding a woman in there?"

The little man purpled. He closed his eyes and swayed, dizzy with sheer fury. When he opened them, he shouted, "Yarrow! If ever I saw an unreal personality, you're it! I don't care how you stand with the hierarchy! I think you're—you're—just not simply *shib!* You've changed. You used to be so humble, so obedient. Now, you're arrogant."

Hal said, evenly at first, his voice rising as he continued, "It wasn't so long ago that you described me as unruly from the day I was born. Suddenly, it seems that I am an example of splendid behavior, one the Sturch may point to with—pardon the cliché—pride. I suggest that I have always behaved as well as could be expected. I suggest that you were and are a picayunish, malicious, nasty, bird-brained pimple on the ass of the Sturch and that you ought to be squeezed until you pop!"

Hal stopped shouting because he was breathing so hard. His heart was hammering; his ears, roaring; his sight, getting dim.

Pornsen backed away, his hands held out before him.

"Hal Yarrow! Hal Yarrow! Control yourself! Forerunner, how you must hate me! And all these years I thought you loved me, that I was your beloved *gapt* and you were my beloved ward. But you hated me. Why?"

The roaring faded away. Hal's vision cleared.

"Are you serious?"

"Of course! I never dreamed, dreamed! Anything that I ever did to you was for you; when I punished you, my heart broke. But I drove myself to it by reminding myself that it was for your good."

Hal laughed and laughed while Pornsen ran down the hall and disappeared into his apartment with a single white-faced look.

Weakly, shaking, Hal leaned against the doorway. This was the most unexpected thing of all. He had been absolutely certain that Pornsen loathed him as a contrary and unnatural monster and that he took a bitter delight in humiliating and whipping him.

Hal shook his head. Surely, the *gapt* was scared and was trying to justify himself.

He unlocked the door and entered. Around and around in his head flew the thought that the courage to speak out against Pornsen had come from Jeannette. Without her, he was nothing, a resentful but scared rabbit. A few hours with her had enabled him to overcome many years of rigid discipline.

He clicked on the front room lights. Looking beyond into the dining room, he could see the closed kitchen door. The rattling of pots came through it. He sniffed deeply.

Steak!

The pleasure was replaced by a frown. He'd told her to hide until he returned. What if he had been a wog or an Uzzite?

When the door swung open, the hinges squeaked. Jeannette's back was to him. At the first protest of unoiled iron, she whirled. The spatula in her hand dropped; the other hand flew to her open mouth.

The angry words on his lips died. If she were to be scolded now, she would probably break out in embarrassing tears.

"*Maw choo!* You startled me!"

He grunted and went by her to lift the lids on the pots.

"You see," she said, her voice trembling as if she divined his anger and were defending herself. "I have lived such a life, being afraid of getting caught, that anything sudden scares me. I am always ready to run."

"How those wogs fooled me!" Hal said sourly. "I thought they were so kind and gentle."

She glanced at him out of the side of her large eyes. Her color had come back; her red lips smiled.

"Oh, they weren't so bad. They really were kind. They gave me everything I wanted, except my freedom. They were afraid I'd make my way back to my sisters."

"What did they care?"

"Oh, they thought there might be some males of my race left in the jungle and that I might give them children. They are terribly frightened of my race becoming numerous and strong again and making war on them. They do not like war."

"They are strange beings," he said. "But we cannot expect to understand those who do not know the reality of the Forerunner. Moreover, they are closer to the insect than to man."

"Being a man does not necessarily mean being better," Jeannette said with a tinge of asperity.

"All God's creatures have their proper place in the universe," he replied. "But man's place is everywhere and everywhen. He can occupy any position in space and can travel in any direction in time. And if he must dispossess a creature to gain that place or time, he is doing only what is right."

"Quoting the Forerunner?"

"Of course."

"Perhaps, he is right. Perhaps. But what is man? Man is a sentient being. A wog is a sentient being. Therefore, the wog is a man. *Nespfa?*"

"*Shib* or *sib,* let's not argue. Why don't we eat?"

"I wasn't arguing."

She smiled and said, "I will set the table. You will see if I can cook or not. There'll be no argument about that."

After the dishes were placed on the table, the two sat down. Hal joined his hands together, put them on the table, bowed his head, and prayed.

"Isaac Sigmen, runner before man, real be your name, we thank you for having made certain this blessed present, which once was the uncertain future. We thank you for this food, which you have actualized from potentiality. We hope and know that you will slay the Backrunner, forestall his wicked attempts to unshake the past and so alter the present. Make this universe solid and real, and omit the fluidity of time. These selves gathered at this table thank you. So be it."

He unfolded his hands and looked at Jeannette. She was staring at him.

Obeying an impulse, he said, "You may pray if you wish."

"Won't you regard my prayer as unreal?"

He hesitated before saying, "Yes. I do not know why I asked you. I certainly would not ask an Israeli or Bantu to pray. I wouldn't eat at the same table with one. But you . . . you are special . . . maybe because unclassified. I . . . I do not know."

"Thank you," she said.

She described a triangle in the air with the middle finger of her right hand. Looking upward, she said, "Great Mother, we thank you."

Hal repressed showing the strange feeling it gave him to hear an unbeliever. He slid open the drawer beneath the table and took out two objects. One he handed to Jeannette. The other he put on his head.

It was a cap with a wide brim from which hung a long veil. It entirely covered his face.

"Put it on," he said to Jeannette.

"Why?"

"So we can't see each other eat, of course," he said impatiently. "There is enough space between the veil and your face for you to manipulate your fork and spoon."

"But why?"

"I told you. So we can't see each other eat."

"Would the sight of me eating make you sick?" she said with a rising inflection.

"Naturally."

"Naturally? Why naturally?"

"Why, eating is so . . . uh . . . I don't know . . . animalistic."

"And have your people always done this? Or did they begin when they found out they were animals?"

"Before the coming of the Forerunner, they ate naked and unashamed. But they were in a state of ignorance."

"Do the Israeli and Bantu hide their faces when they eat?"

"No."

Jeannette rose from the table.

"I cannot eat with this thing over my face. I would feel ashamed."

"But . . . I have to wear my eating cap," he said with a shaky voice. "I couldn't keep my food down."

She spoke a phrase in a language he did not know. But the unfamiliarity did not conceal the bewilderment and hurt.

"I'm sorry," he said. "But that's the way it is. That's the way it should be."

Slowly, she sat down again. She put the cap on.

"Very well, Hal. But I think we must talk about this later. This makes me feel as if I am isolated from you. There is no closeness, no sharing in the good things that life has given us."

"Please don't make any noise while you're eating,"

he said. "And if you must speak, swallow all your food first. I've turned my face when a wog was eating before me, but I couldn't close my ears."

"I'll try not to make you sick," she said. "Just one question. How do you keep your children quiet when they're eating?"

"They never eat with adults. Rather, the only adults at their tables are *gapts*. And these soon teach them the proper behavior."

"Oh."

The meal passed in silence except for the unavoidable sound of cutlery on plate. When Hal finished, he took off his cap.

"Ah, Jeannette, you are a rare cook. The food is so good I almost felt sinful that I should be enjoying it so much. The soup was the best I ever tasted. The bread was delicious. The salad was superb. The steak was perfect."

Jeannette had removed her cap first. Her meal was scarcely touched. Nevertheless, she smiled.

"My aunts trained me well. Among my people, the female is taught at an early age all that will please a man. All."

He laughed nervously and, to cover his uneasiness, lit a cigarette.

Jeannette asked if she might try a cigarette, too.

"Since I am burning, I may as well smoke," she said, and she giggled.

Hal wasn't sure of what she meant, but he laughed to show her that he wasn't angry with her about the eating caps.

Jeannette lit her own cigarette, drew in, coughed, and rushed to the sink for a glass of water. She came back with her eyes streaming, but she at once picked up the cigarette and tried again. In a short time, she was inhaling like a veteran.

"You have amazing imitative powers," Hal said. "I've watched you copying my movements, heard you mimic my speech. Do you know that you pronounce American as well as I do?"

"Show or tell me something once, and you seldom have to do it again. I'm not claiming a superior intelligence, however. As you said, I have an instinct for imitation. Not that I'm not capable of an original thought now and then."

She began chattering lightly and amusingly about her life with her father, sisters, and aunts. Her good spirits seemed genuine; apparently, she was not talking just to conceal the depression caused by the incident at mealtime. She had a trick of raising her eyebrows as she laughed. They were fascinating, almost bracket-shaped. A thin line of black hair rose from the bridge of her nose, turned at right angles, curved slightly while going over the eye sockets, and then made a little hook at the ends.

He asked her if the shape of her eyebrows was a trait of her mother's people. She laughed and replied that she inherited it from her father, the Earthman.

Her laughter was low and musical. It did not get on his nerves, as his ex-wife's had. Lulled by it, he felt pleasant. And every time he thought of how this situation might end and his spirits sagged, he was pulled back into a better mood by something amusing she said. She seemed to be able to anticipate exactly what he needed to blunt any gloominess or sharpen any gaiety.

After an hour, Hal rose to go into the kitchen. On his way past Jeannette, he impulsively ran his fingers through her thick, wavy black hair.

She raised her face and closed her eyes, as if she expected him to kiss her. But, somehow, he could not. He wanted to but just couldn't bring himself to make the first move.

"The dishes will have to be washed," he said. "It would never do for an unexpected visitor to see a table set for two. And another thing we'll have to watch. Keep the cigarettes hidden and the rooms aired out frequently. Now that I've been 'Metered, I'm supposed to have renounced such minor unrealities as smoking."

If Jeannette was disappointed, she did not show it.

She at once busied herself in cleaning up. He smoked and speculated about the chances of getting ginseng tobacco. She so enjoyed the cigarettes that he could not stand the idea of her missing out on them. One of the crewmen with whom he had good relations did not smoke but sold his ration to his mates. Maybe a wog could act as middleman, buy from the sailor, and pass it on to Hal. Fobo might do it, but the whole transaction would have to be handled carefully. Maybe it wasn't worth the risk . . .

Hal sighed. Having Jeannette was wonderful, but she was beginning to complicate his life. Here he was, contemplating a criminal action as if it were the most natural thing in the world.

She was standing before him, hands on her hips, eyes shining.

"Now, Hal, *maw namoo,* if we only had something to drink, it would make a perfect evening."

He got to his feet. "Sorry. I forgot you wouldn't know how to make coffee."

"No. No. It is the liquor I am thinking of. Alcohol, not coffee."

"Alcohol? Great Sigmen, girl, we don't *drink!* That'd be the most disgust—"

He stopped. She was hurt. He mastered himself. After all, she couldn't help it. She came from a different culture. She wasn't even, strictly speaking, all human.

"I'm sorry," he said. "It's a religious matter. Forbidden."

Tears filled her eyes. Her shoulders began to shake. She put her face into her hands and began to sob. "You don't understand. I have to have it. I have to."

"But why?"

She spoke from behind her fingers. "Because during my imprisonment, I had little to do but entertain myself. My captors gave me liquor; it helped to pass the time and make me forget how utterly homesick I was. Before I knew it, I was an—an alcoholic."

Hal clenched his fists and growled, "Those sons of . . . bugs!"

"So you see, I have to have a drink. It would make me feel better, just for the time being. And later, maybe later, I can try to overcome it. I know I can, if you'll help me."

He gestured emptily. "But—but where can I get you some?" His stomach revolted at the idea of trafficking in alcohol. But, if she needed it, he'd try his best to get it.

Swiftly, she said, "Perhaps Fobo could give you some."

"But Fobo was one of your captors! Won't he suspect something if I come asking for alcohol?"

"He'll think it's for you."

"All right," he said, somewhat sullenly, and at the same time guiltily because he was sullen. "But I hate for anybody to think *I* drink. Even if he is just a wog."

She came up to him and seemed to flow against him. Her lips pressed softly. Her body tried to pass through his. He held her for a minute and then took his mouth away.

"Do I have to leave you?" he whispered. "Couldn't you pass up the liquor? Just for tonight? Tomorrow, I'll get you some."

Her voice broke. "Oh, *maw namoo,* I wish I could. How I wish I could. But I can't. I just can't. Believe me."

"I believe you."

He released her and walked into the front room, where he took a hood, cloak, and nightmask out of the closet. His head was bent; his shoulders sagged. Everything would be spoiled. He would not be able to get near her, not with her breath stinking of alcohol. And she'd probably wonder why he was cold, and he wouldn't have the nerve to tell her how revolting she was, because that would hurt her feelings. To make it worse, she'd be hurt anyway if he offered no explanation.

Before he left, she kissed him again on his now frozen lips.

"Hurry! I'll be waiting."

"Yeah."

11

HAL Yarrow knocked lightly on the door of Fobo's apartment. The door did not open at once. No wonder. There was so much noise inside. Hal beat on the door, though reluctantly, for he did not want to attract Pornsen's attention. The *gapt* lived across the hall from Fobo and might open his door to see what was going on. Tonight was not a good time for Pornsen to see him visiting the empathist. Even though Hal had every right to enter a wog's home without being accompanied by a *gapt,* he felt uneasy because of Jeannette. He would not put it past the *gapt* to enter his, Hal's, *puka* while he was gone for a bit of unofficial spying. And, if Pornsen did, he would have Hal. All would be up.

But Hal comforted himself with the thought that Pornsen was not a very brave man. If he took the liberty of entering Hal's place, he would also take the chance of being discovered. And Hal, as a *lamedhian,* could bring so much pressure to bear that Pornsen might not only be disgraced and demoted, he might even be a candidate for H.

Loudly, impatiently, Hal rapped on the door again. This time it swung open. Abasa, Fobo's wife, was smiling at him.

"Hal Yarrow!" she said in Siddo. "Welcome! Why didn't you come in without knocking?"

Hal was shocked. "I couldn't do that!"

"Why not?"

"We just don't do that."

Abasa shrugged her shoulders, but she was too polite to comment. Still smiling, she said, "Well, come on in. I won't bite!"

Hal stepped in and shut the door behind him, though not without a backward glance at Pornsen's door. It was closed.

Inside, the screams of twelve wog children at play bounced off the walls of a room as large as a basketball court. Abasa led Hal across the uncarpeted floor to the opposite end, where a hallway began. They passed by one corner where three wog females, evidently Abasa's visitors, sat at a table. They were occupied in sewing, drinking from tall glasses before them, and chattering. Hal could not understand the few words he could hear; wog females, when talking among themselves, used a vocabulary restricted to their sex. This custom, however, so Hal understood, was swiftly dying out under the impact of increasing urbanization. Abasa's female children were not even learning woman-talk.

Abasa led Hal down to the end of the hall, opened a door, and said, "Fobo, dear! Hal Yarrow, the No-nose, is here!"

Hal, hearing himself so described, smiled. The first time he had met this phrase, he had felt offended. But he had learned that the wogs did not mean it to be insulting.

Fobo came to the door. He was dressed only in a scarlet kilt. Hal could not help thinking for the hundredth time how strange the Ozagen's torso was, with its nippleless chest and the curious construction of shoulder blades attached to the ventral spine. (Would it be called a forebone as opposed to the Earthman's backbone?)

"You are welcome indeed, Hal," said Fobo in Siddo. He switched to American, "Shalom. What happy occasion brings you here? Sit down. I'd offer you a drink, but I'm fresh out."

Hal did not think his dismay showed on his face, but Fobo must have discerned it.

"Anything wrong?"

Hal decided not to waste time. "Yes. Where can I get a quart of liquor?"

"You need some? *Shib.* I will go out with you. The nearest tavern is a low-class hangout; it will give you a chance to see at close range an aspect of Siddo society you doubtless know little about."

The wog went into the closet and returned with an armful of clothes. He put a broad leather belt around his fat stomach and to it fastened a sheath containing a short rapier. Then, he stuck a pistol in the belt. Over his shoulders he fastened a long, kelly green cloak with many black ruffles. On his head he put a dark green skullcap with two artificial antennae. This head covering was the symbol for the Grasshopper clan. Once, it would have been important for a wog of that clan to have always worn it outside his house. Now, the clan system had degenerated to the point where it represented a minor social function, though its political use was still great.

"I need a drink, an alcoholic beverage," Fobo said. "You see, as a professional empathist, I encounter many nerve-racking cases. I give therapy to so many neurotics and psychotics. I must put myself in their shoes, feel their emotions as they feel them. Then I wrench myself out of their shoes and take an objective look at their problems. Through the use of this"— he tapped his head—"and this"—he tapped his nose —"I become them, then become myself, and so, sometimes, enable them to cure themselves."

Hal knew that when Fobo indicated his nose, he meant that the two extremely sensitive antennae inside the projectilelike proboscis could detect the type and flux of his patients' emotions. The odor from a wog's sweat told even more than the expression of his face.

Fobo led Hal down the hall to the big room. He

told Abasa where he was going and affectionately rubbed noses with her.

Then, Fobo handed Hal a mask shaped like a wog's face, and he put his own on. Hal did not ask what it was for. He knew that it was the custom for all Siddo to wear nightmasks. They did serve a utilitarian purpose, for they kept the many biting insects off. Fobo explained their social function.

"We upper-class Siddo keep them on inside when we go—what's the American word?"

"Slumming?" said Hal. "When an upper-class person goes to a lower-class place for amusement?"

"Slumming," said Fobo. "Ordinarily, I do not keep the mask on when I go into a low-class resort, for I go there to have fun with people, not to laugh at them. But, tonight, inasmuch as you are a—I blush to say it, a No-nose—I think it would be more relaxing if you kept the mask on."

When they had walked out of the building, Hal said, "Why the gun and sword?"

"Oh, there isn't too much danger in this—neck of the woods?—but it's best to be careful. Remember what I told you at the ruins? The insects of my planet have developed and specialized far beyond those of your world, according to what you have told me. You know of the parasites and mimics that infest ant colonies? The beetles that look like ants and freeload off the ants because of that resemblance? The pygmy ants and other creatures that live in the walls of the colonies and prey on the eggs and young?

"We have things analogous to those, but they prey off us. Things that hide in sewers or basements or hollow trees or holes in the ground and creep around the city at night. That is why we do not allow our children out after dark. Our streets are well lighted and patrolled, but they are often separated by wooded stretches."

They walked through a park over a path lit with tall lamps that burned gas. Siddo was still in the transition between electricity and the older forms of energy; it

was not unusual to find one area illuminated by light
bulbs, the next by gaslights. Coming out of the park
and onto a broad street, Hal saw other evidences of
Ozagen's culture, the old and the brand new side by
side. Buggies drawn by hoofed animals belonging to
the same subphylum as Fobo and steam-driven
wheeled vehicles. The animals and cars passed over
a thoroughfare covered with tough short-bladed grass
that resisted all efforts to wear it out.

And the buildings were so widely separated that it
was difficult to think of oneself as being in a metropolis. Too bad, thought Hal. The wogs had more than
enough Lebensraum now. But their expanding population made it inevitable that the wide spaces would
be filled with houses and buildings; someday, Ozagen
would be as crowded as Earth.

Then, he corrected himself. Crowded, yes, but not
with wogglebugs. If the *Gabriel* carried out her
planned function, human beings from the Haijac Union
would replace the natives.

He felt a pang at this and also had the thought—
unrealistic, of course—that such an event would be
hideously wrong. What right did beings from another
planet have to come here and callously murder all the
inhabitants?

It was right, because the Forerunner had said so. *Or
was it?*

Fobo said, "Ah, there it is."

He pointed to a building ahead of them. It was
three stories high, shaped something like a ziggurat,
and had arches running from the upper stories to the
ground. These arches had steps on them on which the
residents of the upper stories walked. Like many of
the older Siddo buildings, it had no internal stairways;
the residents went directly from the outside into their
apartments.

However, though old, the tavern on the first story
had a big electric sign blazing above the front door.

"Duroku's Happy Vale," said Fobo, translating the
ideograms.

The bar was in the basement. Hal, after stopping to shudder at the blast of liquor fumes that came up the steps, followed the wog. He paused in the entrance.

Strong odors of alcohol mingled with loud bars of a strange music and even louder talk. Wogs crowded the hexagonal-topped tables and leaned across big pewter steins to shout in each other's face. Somebody waved his hands uncoordinatedly and sent a stein crashing. A waitress hurried up with a towel to mop up the mess. When she bent over, she was slapped resoundingly on the rump by a jovial, green-faced, and very fat wogglebug. His tablemates howled with laughter, their broad V-in-V lips wide open. The waitress laughed, too, and said something to the fat one that must have been witty, for those at the neighboring tables guffawed.

On a platform at one end of the room a five-piece band slammed out fast and weird notes. Hal saw three instruments that looked Terranlike: a harp, a trumpet, and a drum. A fourth musician, however, was not producing any music himself, but he was now and then prodding with a long stick a rat-sized locustoid creature in a cage. When so urged, the insect rubbed its hind wings over its back legs and gave four loud chirps followed by a long, nerve-scratching screech.

The fifth player was pumping away at a bellows connected to a bag and three short and narrow pipes. A thin squealing came out.

Fobo shouted, "Don't think that noise is typical of our music. It's cheap, popular stuff. I'll take you to a symphony concert one of these days, and you'll hear what great music is like."

The wog led the man to one of the curtained-off booths scattered along the walls. They sat down. A waitress came to them. Sweat ran off her forehead and down her tubular nose.

"Keep your mask on until we've gotten our drinks," said Fobo. "Then we can close the curtains."

The waitress said something in Wog.

Fobo repeated in American for Hal's benefit. "Beer,

wine, or beetlejuice. Myself, I wouldn't touch the first two. They're for women and children."

Hal didn't want to lose face. He said, with a bravado he didn't feel, "The latter, of course."

Fobo held up two fingers. The waitress returned quickly with two big steins. The wog leaned his nose into the fumes and breathed deeply. He closed his eyes in ecstasy, lifted the stein, and drank a long time. When he put the container down, he belched loudly and then smacked his lips.

"Tastes as good coming up as going down!" he bellowed.

Hal felt queasy. He had been whipped too many times as a child for his uninhibited eructations.

"But Hal," said Fobo, "you are not drinking!"

Yarrow said weakly, *"Damif'ino,"* Siddo for, "I hope this doesn't hurt," and he drank.

Fire ran down his throat like lava down a volcano's slope. And, like a volcano, Hal erupted. He coughed and wheezed; liquor spurted out of his mouth; his eyes shut and squeezed out big tears.

"Very good, isn't it?" said Fobo calmly.

"Ycs, vcry good," croaked Yarrow from a throat that seemed to be permanently scarred. Though he had spat most of the stuff out, some of it must have dropped straight through his intestines and into his legs, for he felt a hot tide down there swinging back and forth as if pulled by some invisible moon circling around and around in his head, a big moon that bulged and brushed against the inside of his skull.

"Have another."

The second drink he managed better—outwardly, at least, for he did not cough or sputter. But inwardly he was not so unconcerned. His belly writhed, and he was sure he would disgrace himself. After a few deep breaths, he thought he would keep the liquor down. Then, he belched. The lava got as far as his throat before he managed to stop it.

"Pardon me," he said, blushing.

"Why?" said Fobo.

Hal thought that was one of the funniest retorts he had ever heard. He laughed loudly and sipped at the stein. If he could empty it swiftly and then buy a quart for Jeannette, he could get back before the night was completely wasted.

When the liquor had receded halfway down the stein, Hal heard Fobo, dimly and far-off as if he were at the end of a long tunnel, ask him if he cared to see where the alcohol was made.

"Shib," Hal said.

He rose but had to put a hand on the table to steady himself. The wog told him to put his mask back on.

"Earthmen are still objects of curiosity. We don't want to waste all evening answering questions. Or drinking drinks that'll be forced on us."

They threaded through the noisy crowd to a back room. There Fobo gestured and said, "Behold! The *kesarubu!"*

Hal looked. If he had not had some of his inhibitions washed away in the liquorish flood, he might have been overwhelmingly repulsed. As it was, he was curious.

The thing sitting on a chair by the table might, at first glance, have been taken for a wogglebug. It had the blond fuzz, the bald pate, the nose, and the V-shaped mouth. It also had the round body and enormous paunch of some of the Ozagens.

But a second look in the bright light from the unshaded bulb overhead showed a creature whose body was sheathed in a hard and light green tinted chitin. And, though it wore a long cloak, the legs and arms were naked. They were not smooth-skinned but were ringed, segmented with the edges of armor-sections, like stovepipes.

Fobo spoke to it. Yarrow understood some of the words; the others, he was able to fill in.

"Ducko, this is Mr. Yarrow. Say hello to Mr. Yarrow, Ducko."

The big blue eyes looked at Hal. There was nothing

about them to distinguish them from a wog's, yet they seemed inhuman, thoroughly arthropodal.

"Hello, Mr. Yarrow," Ducko said in a parrot's voice.

"Tell Mr. Yarrow what a fine night it is."

"It's a fine night, Mr. Yarrow."

"Tell him Ducko is happy to see him."

"Ducko is happy to see you."

"And serve him."

"And serve you."

"Show Mr. Yarrow how you make beetlejuice."

A wog standing by the table glanced at his wristwatch. He spoke in rapid Ozagen. Fobo translated.

"He says Ducko ate a half hour ago. He should be ready to serve. These creatures eat a big meal every half hour and then they—watch!"

Duroku set on the table a huge earthenware bowl. Ducko leaned over it until a half-inch-long tube projecting from his chest was poised above the edge of the bowl. The projection, thought Hal, was probably a modified tracheal opening. From the tube a clear liquid shot into the bowl until it was filled to the brim. Duroku grabbed the bowl and carried it off. An Ozagen came from the kitchen with a plate of what Hal later found out was highly sugared spaghetti. He set it down, and Ducko began eating from it with a big spoon.

Hal's brain was by then not working very fast, but he began to see what was going on. Frantically, he looked around for a place to vomit. Fobo shoved a drink under his nose. For lack of anything better to do, he swallowed some. Whole hog or none. Surprisingly, the fiery stuff settled his stomach. Or else burned away the rising tide.

"Exactly," replied Fobo to Hal's strangled question. "These creatures are a superb example of parasitical mimicry. Though quasi-insectal, they look much like us. They live among us and earn their room and board by furnishing us with a cheap and smooth alcoholic drink. You noticed its enormous belly, *shib?* It is there that they so rapidly manufacture the alcohol and so easily upchuck it. Simple and natural, yes? Duroku has two others working for him, but it is their night off, and doubtless they are in some neighborhood tavern, getting drunk. A sailor's holiday—"

Hal burst out, "Can't we buy a quart and get out? I feel sick. It must be the closeness of the air. Or something."

"Something, probably," Fobo murmured.

He sent a waitress after two quarts. While they were waiting for her, they saw a short wog in a mask and blue cloak enter. The newcomer stood in the doorway, black boots widespread and the long tubular projection of the mask pointing this way and that like a sub's periscope peering for prey.

Hal gasped and said, "Pornsen! I can see his uniform under the cloak!"

"*Shib,*" replied Fobo. "That drooping shoulder and the black boots also give him away. Who does he think he's fooling?"

Hal looked wildly around. "I've got to get out of here!"

The waitress returned with the bottles. Fobo paid her and gave one to Hal, who automatically put it in the inside pocket of his cloak.

The *gapt* saw them through the doorway, but he must not have recognized them. Yarrow wore his mask, while the empathist probably looked to Pornsen like any other wog. Methodical as always, Pornsen evidently was determined to make a thorough search. He brought up his sloping shoulder in a sudden gesture and began parting the curtains of the booths along the walls. Whenever he saw a wog with his or her mask still on, he lifted the grotesque covering and looked behind.

Fobo chuckled, and he said, in American, "He won't keep that up long. What does he think we Siddo are? A bunch of mouses?"

What he had been waiting for happened. A burly wog suddenly stood up as Pornsen reached for his mask and instead lifted the *gapt's*. Surprised at seeing the non-Ozagenian features, the wog stared for a second. Then, he gave a screech, yelled something, and punched the Earthman in the nose.

At once, there was bedlam. Pornsen staggered back into a table, knocking it and its steins over, and fell to the floor. Two wogs jumped him. Another hit a fourth. The fourth struck back. Duroku, carrying a short club, ran up and began thumping his fighting customers on the backs and legs. Somebody threw beetlejuice in his face.

And, at that moment, Fobo threw the switch that plunged the tavern into darkness.

Hal stood bewildered. A hand seized his. "Follow me!" The hand tugged. Hal turned and allowed himself to be led, stumbling, toward what he thought was the back door.

Any number of others must have had the same idea. Hal was knocked down and trampled upon. Fobo's hand was torn from his. Yarrow cried out for the wog, but any possible answer was drowned out in a chorus of *Beat it! Get off my back, you dumb son-of-a-bug! Great Larva, we're piled up in the doorway!*

Sharp reports added to the noise. A foul stench choked Hal as the wogs, under nervous stress, released the gas in their madbags. Gasping, Hal fought his way through the door. A few seconds later, his mad scrambling over twisting bodies earned him his freedom. He lurched down an alleyway. Once on the street, he ran as fast as he could. He didn't know where he was going. His one thought was to put as much distance as possible between himself and Pornsen.

Arc lights on top of tall, slender iron poles flashed by. He ran with his shoulder almost scraping the buildings. He wanted to stay in the shadows thrown by the many balconies jutting out from above. After a minute, he slowed down at a narrow passageway. A glance showed him it wasn't a blind alley. He darted down it until he came to a large square can, one that by its odor must have been used for garbage. Squatting behind it, he tried to lessen his gaspings. Presently, his lungs regained their balance; he no longer had to sob for air. He could listen without having his heart thudding in his ears.

He heard no pursuer. After a while, he decided it was safe to rise. He felt the bottle in his cloak pocket. Miraculously, it had not been broken. Jeanette would get her liquor. What a story he would have to tell her! After all he had gone through for her, he would surely get a just reward . . .

He shivered with goose pimples at the thought and began to walk briskly down the alley. He had no idea where he was, but he carried a map of the city in his pocket. It had been printed in the ship and bore street names in Ozagen with American and Icelandic translations beneath. All he had to do was read the street signs under one of the many lamps, orient himself with the map, and return home. As for Pornsen, the fellow had no real evidence against him and would not be able to accuse him until he got some. Hal's golden *lamedh* made him above suspicion. Pornsen . . .

12

PORNSEN! No sooner had he muttered the name than the flesh appeared. There was a click of hard boot heels behind him. He turned. A short, cloaked figure was coming down the alley. A lamp's glow outlined the droop of a shoulder and shone on black leather boots. His mask was off.

"Yarrow!" shrilled the *gapt*, triumphantly. "No use running! I saw you in that tavern. You won't be able to save yourself now!"

He click-clacked up to his ward's tall rigid form. "Drinking! I know you were drinking!"

"Yeah?" Hal croaked. "What else?"

"Isn't that enough?" screamed the *gapt*. "Or are you hiding something in your apartment? Maybe you are! Maybe you've got the place filled with bottles. Come on! Let's get back to your apartment. We'll go over it and see what we see. I wouldn't be surprised to find all sorts of evidence of your unreal thinking."

Hal hunched his shoulders and clenched his fists, but he said nothing. When he was told by the *gapt* to precede him back to Fobo's building, he walked without a sign of resistance. Like conqueror and conquered, they marched from the alley into the street. Yarrow, however, spoiled the picture by reeling a little and having to put his hand to the wall to steady himself.

Pornsen sneered. "You drunken *joat!* You make me sick to my stomach!"

Hal pointed ahead. "I'm not the only one who's sick. Look at that fellow."

He was not really interested, but he had a wild hope that anything he said or did, however trivial, might put off the final and fatal moment when they would return to his apartment. He was pointing at a large and evidently intoxicated wogglebug hanging onto a lamppost to keep from falling on his needle-shaped nose. He might have been a nineteenth- or twentieth-century drunk, complete to top hat, cloak, and lamppost. Now and then, the creature groaned as if he were deeply disturbed.

"Perhaps we'd better stop to see if he's hurt," said Hal.

He had to say something, anything to delay Pornsen. Before his captor could protest, he went up to the wog. He put his hand on the free arm—the other was wrapped around the post—and spoke in Siddo.

"Can we help you?"

The big wog looked as if he, too, had been in a brawl. His cloak, besides being ripped down the back, was spotted with dried green blood. He kept his face away from Hal, so that the Earthman had a hard time understanding his muttering.

Pornsen jerked at his arm. "Come on, Yarrow. He'll get by all right. What's one sick bug more or less?"

"*Shib,*" agreed Hal tonelessly. He let his hand drop and started to walk on. Pornsen, behind, took one step and then bumped into Hal as Hal stopped.

"What are you stopping for, Yarrow?" The *gapt's* voice was suddenly apprehensive.

And then the voice was screaming in agony.

Hal whirled—to see in grim actuality what had flashed across his mind and caused him to stop in his tracks. When he had put his hand on the wog's arm, he had felt, not warm skin, but hard and cool chitin. For a few seconds, the meaning of that had not cleared the brain's switchboard. Then it had come through, and he had remembered the talk he and Fobo had had on the way to the tavern, and why Fobo wore a sword. Too late, he had wheeled to warn Pornsen.

Now the *gapt* was holding both hands to his eyes and shrieking. The big thing that had been leaning against the lamppost was advancing toward Hal. Its body seemed to grow huger with every step. A sac across its chest swelled until it looked like a palpitating gray balloon and a wheezing sound accompanied its deflation. The hideous insectal face, with two vestigial arms waving on each side of its mouth and the funnel-shaped proboscis below the mouth, was pointed at him. It was that proboscis which Hal had mistakenly thought was a wog's nose. In reality, the thing must have breathed through tracheae and two slits below the enormous eyes. Normally, its breath must saw loudly through the slits, but it must have suppressed the sound in order not to warn its victims.

Hal yelled with fright. At the same time he grabbed his cloak and threw it up before his face. His mask might have saved him, but he did not care to take the chance.

Something burned the back of his hand. He yelped with pain but leaped forward. Before the thing could breathe in air to bloat the sac again and expel the acid through the funnel, Hal rammed his head against its paunch.

The thing said, "Oof!" and fell backward where it lay on its back and thrashed its legs and arms like a giant poisonous bug—which it was. Then, as it recovered from the shock and rolled over and tried to get back on its feet, Hal kicked hard. His leather toe drove with a crunching sound through the thin chitin.

The toe withdrew; blood, dark in the lamplight, oozed out; Hal kicked again in the open place. The thing screamed and tried to crawl away on all fours. The Terran leaped upon it with both feet and drove it sprawling to the cement. He pressed his heel against its thin neck and shoved with all the strength of his leg. The neck cracked, and the thing lay still. Its lower

jaw dropped open and exposed two rows of tiny needle teeth. The mouth's rudimentary arms wigwagged
feebly for a while and then drooped.

Hal's chest heaved in agony. He couldn't get
enough air. His guts quivered and threatened to force
their way through his throat. Then they did, and Hal
bent over, retching.

All at once, he was sober. By that time Pornsen had
quit screaming. He was lying huddled on his side in
the gutter. Hal turned him over and shuddered at what
he saw. The eyes were partly burned out, and the lips
were gray with large blisters. The tongue, sticking
from the mouth, was swollen and lumpy. Evidently,
Pornsen had swallowed some of the venom.

Hal straightened up and walked away. A wog pa-
trol would find the *gapt's* body and turn it over to the
Earthmen. Let the hierarchy figure out what had happened. Pornsen was dead, and now that he was, Yarrow admitted to himself what he had never allowed
himself to admit before this time. He had hated Pornsen. And he was glad that he was dead. If Pornsen
had suffered horribly, so what? His pains were brief,
but the pain and grief he had caused Hal had lasted
for almost thirty years.

A sound behind him made him whirl around.

"Fobo?"

There was a moan, followed by pain-garbled words.
"Pornsen? You can't be . . . you're . . . dead."

But Pornsen was alive. He was standing up, sway-
ing.

He held his hands out before him to feel his way
and took a few weak, exploratory steps.

For a moment, Hal was so panicked he thought of
running away. But he forced himself to remain rooted
and to think rationally.

If the wogs did find Pornsen, they'd turn him over
to the doctors of the *Gabriel*. And the doctors would
give Pornsen new eyes from the meat bank and would
inject regeneratives into him. In two weeks, Pornsen's

tongue would grow out again. And he'd talk. Forerunner, how he'd talk!

Two weeks? *Now!* There was nothing to prevent Pornsen from writing.

Pornsen groaned with physical pain; Hal, with mental.

There was only one thing to do.

He went up to Pornsen and seized his hand. The *gapt* flinched and said something unintelligible.

"It's Hal," said Yarrow.

Pornsen reached out his free hand and pulled a notebook and pen from his pocket. Hal released the other hand. Pornsen wrote on the paper and then handed the notebook to Hal.

The moonlight was bright enough to read by. The handwriting was a scrawl, but, even blind, Pornsen could write legibly.

Take me to the *Gabriel*, son. I swear by the Forerunner I won't say a word about the liquor to anybody. I'll be eternally grateful. But don't leave me here in my pain at the mercy of monsters. I love you.

Hal patted Pornsen on the shoulder and said, "Take my hand. I'll lead you."

At the same time, he heard a noise from down the street. A group of noisy wogs was heading his way.

He pulled Pornsen into the nearby park, guiding the stumbling man around the trees and bushes. After they'd walked a hundred yards, they came to an especially thick grouping of trees. Hal halted. Unfamiliar sounds were coming from the center of the grove—clicking and wheezing sounds.

He peered around a tree and saw the origin of the noise. The bright moonlight fell on the corpse of a wog, or, rather, on what was left of it. The upper part was stripped of flesh. Around it and on it were many silvery-white insects. These resembled ants but were at least a foot high. The clicking came from their mandibles working on the corpse. The wheezing came from the air sacs on their heads breathing in and out.

Hal had thought he was hidden, but they must have detected him. Suddenly, they had disappeared into the shadows of the trees on the side of the grove opposite him.

He hesitated, then decided that they were scavengers and would give a healthy person no trouble. Probably, the wog was a drunk who had passed out and been killed by the ants.

He led Pornsen to the corpse and examined it because this was his first chance to inspect the bone structure of the indigenes. The spinal column of the wog was located in the anterior of the torso. It rose from unhumanly shaped hips in a curve that was the mirror image of the curve of a man's spine. However, two sacs of the intestinal tract lay on each side of the spine, forward of the hips. They made a stomach with a hollow in its center. The stomach of a live wog concealed the depression, for the skin stretched tightly over it.

Such an internal construction was to be expected in a being that had developed from the ancestors similar to those of the insects. Hundreds of millions of years ago, the ancestors of the wogs had been unspecialized, wormlike prearthropods. But evolution had intended to make a sentient being from the worm. And, realizing the limitations of true arthropods, evolution had split the wogs' Nth-great-grandfather from the phylum of Arthropoda. When the crustacea, arachnida, and insecta had formed exoskeletons and many legs, Grandfather Wog the Nth had not gone along with them. He had refused to harden his delicate cuticle skin into chitin. Instead, he had erected a skeleton inside the flesh. But his central nervous system was still ventral, and the feat of shifting spinal nerves and spine from front to back was beyond him. So, he had formed the spine where it had to be. And the rest of his skeleton had to go along. The inner parts of a wog were unmistakably different from a mammal's. But if the form was different, the function was similar.

Hal would have liked to investigate further, but he had work to do.

Work which he hated.

Pornsen wrote something in the notebook and handed it to Hal.

Son, I am in terrible pain. Please don't hesitate about taking me to the ship. I will not betray you. Have I ever broken a promise to you? I love you.

Hal thought, *The only promise you ever made to me was to whip me.*

He looked at the shadows between the trees. The pale bodies of the ants were like a forest of mushrooms. Waiting until he left.

Pornsen mumbled something and sat down on the grass. His head drooped.

"Why do I have to do this?" murmured Hal.

He thought, *I don't have to. Jeannette and I could throw ourselves on the mercy of the wogs. Fobo would be the one to go to. The wogs could hide us. But would they do it? If I could be sure. But I can't. They might surrender us to the Uzzites.*

"No use putting it off," he murmured.

He groaned, and he said, "Why must I do this? Why couldn't he have died back there?"

He drew a long knife from a sheath in his boot.

At that moment, Pornsen raised his head and looked upward with scarred eyes. His hand groped for Hal. A ghastly caricature of a smile formed on his burned lips.

Hal raised his knife until its point was about six inches from Pornsen's throat.

"Jeannette, I am doing this for you!" Hal said loudly.

But the knifepoint did not move, and, after a few seconds, it dropped.

"I can't do it," Hal said. "Can't."

Yet, he must do something, something which would either keep Pornsen from informing on him or would remove him and Jeannette from the scene of danger.

Moreover, he had to see that Pornsen was given medical care. The suffering of the man was making him sick, making him writhe with empathy. If he could have killed Pornsen, he would have put an end to that suffering. But he could not do it.

Pornsen, mumbling with burned lips, took a few steps forward, his hands held out at chest level and rotating as he felt for Hal. Hal stepped to one side. He was thinking furiously. There was only one course of action. That was to get Jeannette and make a run for it. His first thought to get a wog to take Pornsen to the ship was discarded. Pornsen would have to be in agony for a while. Hal needed every second of time he could get, and to try to ease the *gapt's* pain quickly would be treachery to Jeannette—not to mention himself.

Pornsen had been walking slowly forward, exploring the air with his hands, shuffling his feet across the grass so he wouldn't stumble over an obstacle. Presently, his foot came into contact with the bones of the native. He halted, and he stooped to feel. When he closed his hands around the ribs and pelvis, he froze. For several seconds, he kept his stance, then he began feeling the length of the skeleton. His fingers touched the skull, moved around it, tested the fragments of flesh clinging to it.

Abruptly, seemingly terrified, perhaps realizing that whatever had stripped the wog of flesh might be close and that he was helpless, he straightened up and ran headlong. A choking scream came from him as he sped across the glade. The high-pitched ululation ended abruptly. He had rammed into a tree trunk and fallen on his back.

Before he could rise, he was overwhelmed by a wheezing and clicking horde of mushroom-white bodies.

Hal did not think of the fact that he was not be-having rationally. Instead, giving a cry, he ran toward the ants. Halfway across the glade, Hal saw them dis-appear into the shadows, but not so far that he could not discern their massed whiteness.

Reaching Pornsen, Hal sank down to one knee and examined him.

In those few moments, the man's clothing had been torn to shreds and his flesh bitten in many places.

His eyes stared straight upward; his jugular vein had been severed.

Hal, moaning, rose and walked swiftly from the grove. Behind him was a rustling and wheezing as the ants surged forward from the protection of the trees. Hal did not look back.

And, when he stepped under the light of the street-lamp, the pressure inside him found vent. Tears ran down his cheeks. His shoulders shook with sobs. He staggered like a drunk. His intestines felt as if they were being pulled apart.

He did not know if it was grief or if it was hate at last finding expression because the cause of his hate could no longer retaliate against him. Perhaps, it was both grief and hate. Whatever it was, it was working out of his body like a poison; his body was expelling it. At the same time, it was boiling him alive.

Yet, it was coming out. Though he felt he was dy-ing, by the time he had walked to his home, he was rid of the poison. Fatigue leadened his arms and legs, and he could scarcely find the energy to walk up the flight of steps to the front door of the building.

At the same time, his heart felt light. It was strong, pumping unimpeded as if a hand around it had re-leased its clutch.

13

A tall ghost in a light blue shroud was waiting for the Terran in the false dawn. It was Fobo, the empathist, standing in the hexagonal-shaped arch that led into his building. He threw back the hood and exposed a face that was scratched on one cheek and blackened around the right eye.

He chuckled and said, "Some son-of-a-bug pulled my mask off and plowed me good. But it was fun. It helps if you blow off steam now and then. How did you come out? I was afraid you might have been picked up by the police. Normally, that wouldn't worry me, but I know your colleagues at the ship would frown upon such activities."

Hal smiled wanly.

"Frown misses it by a mile."

He wondered how Fobo knew what the hierarch's reactions would be. How much did these wogs know about the Terrestrials? Were they onto the Haijac game and waiting to pounce? If so, with what? Their technology, as far as could be determined, was far behind Earth's. True, they seemed to know more of psychic functions than the Terrans did, but that was understandable. The Sturch had long ago decreed that the proper psychology had been perfected and that further research was unnecessary. The result had been a standstill in the psychical sciences.

He shrugged mentally. He was too tired to think of such things. All he wanted was to go to bed.

"I'll tell you later what happened."

Fobo replied, "I can guess. Your hand. You'd better let me fix that burn. Nightlifer venom is nasty."

Like a little child, Hal followed him to the wog's apartment and let him put a cooling salve on it.

"*Shib* as *shib*," Fobo said. "Go to bed. Tomorrow you can tell me all about it."

Hal thanked him and walked down to his floor. His hand fumbled with the key. Finally, after using Sigmen's name in vain, he inserted the key. When he had shut and locked the door, he called Jeannette. She must have been hiding in the closet-within-a-closet in the bedroom, for he heard two doors bang. In a moment she was running to him. She threw her arms around him.

"Oh, *maw num, maw num!* What has happened? I was so worried. I thought I would scream when the night went by, and you didn't return."

Though he was sorry he had caused her pain, he could not help a prickling of pleasure because she cared enough about him to worry. Mary, perhaps, might have been sympathetic, but she would have felt duty-bound to repress it and to lecture him on his unreal thinking and the resulting injury to himself.

"There was a brawl."

He had decided not to say anything about the *gapt* or the nightlifer. Later, when the strain had passed, he'd talk.

She untied his cloak and hood and took off his mask. She hung them up in the front room closet, and he sank into a chair and closed his eyes.

A moment later, they were opened by the sound of liquid pouring into a glass. She was standing in front of him and filling a large glass from the quart. The odor of beetlejuice began to turn his stomach, and the picture of a beautiful girl about to drink the nauseating stuff spun it all the way around.

She looked at him. The delicate brackets of her brows rose.

"*Kyetil?*"

"Nothing's the matter!" he groaned. "I'm all right."

She put down the glass, picked up his hand, and led him into the bedroom. There she gently sat him down, pressed on his shoulders until he lay down, and then took off his shoes. He didn't resist. After she unbuttoned his shirt, she stroked his hair.

"You're sure you're all right?"

"*Shib*. I could lick the world with one hand tied behind my back."

"Good."

The bed creaked as she got up and walked out of the room. He began to drift into sleep, but her return awakened him. Again, he opened his eyes. She was standing with a glass in her hand.

She said, "Would you like a sip now, Hal?"

"Great Sigmen, don't you understand?" Fury roused him and he sat up.

"Why do you think I got sick? I can't stand the stuff! I can't stand to see you drink it. It makes me sick. You make me sick. What's the matter with you? Are you stupid?"

Jeannette's eyes widened. Blood drained from her face and left the pigment of her lips a crimson moon in a white lake. Her hand shook so that the liquor spilled.

"Why—why—" she gasped—"I thought you said you felt fine. I thought you were all right. I thought you wanted to go to bed with me."

Yarrow groaned. He shut his eyes and lay back down. Sarcasm was lost on her. She insisted on taking everything literally. She would have to be reeducated. If he weren't so exhausted, he would have been shocked by her open proposal—so much like that of the Scarlet Woman in *The Western Talmud* when she had tried to seduce the Forerunner.

But he was past being shocked. Moreover, a voice on the edge of his conscience said that she had merely put into hard and unrecallable words what he had planned in his heart all this time. But when they were spoken!

A crash of glass shattered his thoughts. He jerked upright. She was standing there, face twisted, lovely red mouth quivering, and tears flowing. Her hand was empty. A large wet patch against the wall, still dripping, showed what had become of the glass.

"I thought you loved me!" she shouted.

Unable to think of anything to say, he stared. She spun and walked away. He heard her go into the front room and begin to sob loudly. Unable to endure the sound, he jumped out of bed and walked swiftly after her. These rooms were supposed to be soundproof, but one never knew. What if she were overheard?

Anyway, she was twisting something inside him, and he had to straighten it out.

When he entered the front room, he saw she was looking downcast. For a while, he stood silent, wanting to say something but utterly unable to because he had never been forced to solve such a problem before. Haijac women didn't cry often, and if they did, they wept alone in privacy.

He sat down by her and put his hand on her soft shoulder.

"Jeannette."

She turned quickly and laid her dark hair against his chest. She said, between sobs, "I thought maybe you didn't love me. And I couldn't stand it. Not after all I've been through!"

"Well, Jeannette, I didn't—I mean—I wasn't . . . "

He paused. He had had no intention of saying he loved her. He'd never told any woman he loved her, not even Mary. Nor had any woman ever told him. And here was this woman on a faraway planet, only half-human at that, taking it for granted that he was hers, body and self.

He began speaking in a soft voice. Words came easily because he was quoting Moral Lecture AT-16:

" ' . . . all beings with their hearts in the right place are brothers . . . Man and woman are brother and sister . . . Love is everywhere . . . but love . . . should be on a higher plane . . . Man and woman should rightly loathe the beastly act as something the Great Mind, the Cosmic Observer, has not yet eliminated in man's evolutionary development . . . The time will come when children will be produced through thought alone. Meanwhile, we must recognize sex as necessary for only one reason: children . . .'"

Slap! His head rang, and points of fire whirled off into the blackness before his eyes.

It was a moment before he could realize that Jeannette had leaped to her feet and slammed him hard with the palm of her hand. He saw her standing above him with her eyes slitted and her red mouth open and drawn back in a snarl.

Then, she whirled and ran into the bedroom. He got up and followed her. She was lying on the bed, sobbing.

"Jeannette, you don't understand!"

"Fva tuh fe fu'!"

When he understood that, he blushed. Then he became furious. He grabbed her by the shoulder and turned her over so that she faced him.

Suddenly he was saying, "But I do love you, Jeannette. I *do*."

He sounded strange, even to himself. The concept of love, as she meant it, was alien to him—rusty, perhaps, if it could be put that way. It would need much polishing. But it would, he knew, be polished. Here in his arms was one whose very nature and instinct and education were pointed toward love.

He had thought he had drained himself of grief earlier that night; but now, as he forgot his resolve not to tell her what had happened, and as he recounted, step by step, the long and terrible night, tears ran down his face. Thirty years made a deep well; it took a long time to pump out all the weeping.

Jeannette, too, cried, and said that she was sorry that she had gotten angry at him. She promised never again to do so. He said it was all right. They kissed again and again until, like two babies who have wept themselves and loved themselves out of frustration and fury, they passed gently into sleep.

14 ✂

AT 0900 Ship's Time, Yarrow walked into the *Gabriel,* the scent of morning dew on the grass in his nostrils. As he had a little time before the conference, he looked up Turnboy, the historian *joat.* Casually, he asked Turnboy if he knew anything of a space flight emigration from France after the Apocalyptic War. Turnboy was delighted to show off his knowledge. Yes, the remnants of the Gallic nation had gathered in the Loire country after the Apocalyptic War and had formed the nucleus of what might have become a new France.

But the swiftly growing colonies sent from Iceland to the northern part of France, and from Israel to the southern part, had surrounded the Loire. New France found itself squeezed economically and religiously. Sigmen's disciples invaded the territory in waves of missionaries. High tariffs strangled the little state's trade. Finally, a group of Frenchmen, seeing the inevitable absorption or conquest of their state, religion, and tongue, had left in six rather primitive spaceships to find another Gaul rotating about some far-off star. It was highly improbable that they had succeeded.

Hal thanked Turnboy and walked to the conference room. He spoke to many. Half of them, like him, had a Mongolian tinge to their features. They were the English-speaking descendants of Hawaiian and Aus-

tralian survivors of the same war which had deci-
mated France. Their many-times great-grandfathers
had repopulated Australia, the Americas, Japan, and
China.

Almost half of the crew spoke Icelandic. Their ancestors had sailed from the grim island to spread across
northern Europe, Siberia, and Manchuria.

About a sixteenth of the crew knew Georgian as
their native tongue. Their foreparents had moved down
from the Caucasus Mountains and resettled depopu-
lated southern Russia, Bulgaria, northern Iran, and
Afghanistan.

The conference was a memorable one. First, Hal
was moved from twentieth place to the Archurielite's
left to sixth from his right. The *lamedh* on his chest
made the difference. Second, there was little difficulty
about Pornsen's death. The *gapt* was considered a
casualty of the undeclared war. Everyone was warned,
again, about the nightlifers and other things that sometimes prowled Siddo after dusk. It was not, however,
suggested that the Haijacs quit their moonlit espionage.

Macneff ordered Hal, as the dead *gapt's* spiritual
son, to arrange for the funeral the following day. Then
he pulled down a huge map from a long roller on the
wall. This was the representation of Earth that would
be given to the wogs.

It was a good example of the Haijacs' subtlety and
Chinese box-within-a-box thinking. The two hemi-
spheres of Earth were depicted on the map with
colored political boundaries. It was correct as far as
the Bantu and Malay states were concerned. But the
positions of the Israeli and Haijac nations had been
reversed. The legend beneath the map indicated that
green was the color of the Forerunner states and yellow the Hebrew states. The green portion, however,
was a ring around the Mediterranean, and a broad
band covering Arabia, the southern half of Asia Minor,
and northern India.

In other words, if, by an inconceivable chance, the
Ozagen succeeded in capturing the *Gabriel* and built

ships with it as a model, and used the navigational data aboard to find Sol, they would still attack the wrong country. Undoubtedly, they would not bother to contact personally the people of Earth, for they would want to use the element of surprise. Thus, the Israeli would never get a chance to explain before the bombs went off. And the Haijac Union, warned, would hurl its space fleet against the invaders.

"However," said Macneff, "I do not think that the pseudofuture I have just suggested could ever become reality. Not unless the Backrunner is more powerful than I believe. Of course, you could take the attitude that this course might be best. What better shape could the future take than to wipe out our Israeli enemies through means of these nonhumans?

"But, as you all know, our ship is well guarded against attack by open assault or stealth. Our radar, lasers, audiodetection equipment, and starlight scopes are operating at all times. Our weapons are ready. The wogs are inferior in technology; they have nothing to bring against us that we could not easily crush.

"Nevertheless, if the Backrunner were to inspire them to superhuman cunning, and they did get into the ship, they would fail. If the wogs should reach a certain point in the ship, one of two officers always on duty on the bridge will press a button. This will wipe out all navigational data in the memory banks; the wogs will never be able to locate Sol.

"And if the wogs—Sigmen forbid—should reach the bridge, then the officer on duty there will press another button."

Macneff paused and looked at those around the conference table. Most of them were pale, for they knew what he was going to say.

"An H-bomb will utterly destroy this ship. It will also annihilate the city of Siddo. And we will be honored forever in the eyes of the Forerunner and the Sturch.

"Naturally, we would all prefer that this not happen. And I wish I could warn Siddo so that they would not dare to attack. However, to do so would spoil our present good relations with them and might result in our having to launch Project Ozagenocide before we are ready."

After the conference, Hal gave orders for the funeral arrangements. Other duties kept him till dark, when he returned home.

When Hal locked the door behind him, he heard the shower running. He hung his coat up in the closet; the water stopped splashing. As he went toward his bedroom door, Jeannette stepped out from the bathroom. She was drying her hair with a big towel, and she was naked.

She said, *"Baw yoo,* Hal," and walked into the bedroom, unselfconsciously. Feebly, Hal replied. He turned and went back into the front room. He felt foolish because of his timorousness and, at the same time, vaguely wicked, unreal, because of the pounding of his heart, his heavy breathing, the hot and fluid fingers that wrapped themselves, half-pain, half-delight, around his loins.

She came out dressed in a pale green robe which he had bought for her and which she had recut and resewn to fit her figure. Her heavy black hair was piled on her head in a Psyche knot. She kissed him and asked if he wanted to come into the kitchen while she cooked. He said that would be fine.

She began making a sort of spaghetti. He asked her to tell him about her life. Once started, she was not hard to keep going.

". . . and so my father's people found a planet like Earth and settled there. It was a beautiful planet; that is why they called it *Wuhbopfey,* the beautiful land.

"According to my father, there are about thirty million living there on one continent. My father was not content to live the life his grandfathers had lived— tilling the soil or running a shop and raising many children. He and some other young men like him took the only spaceship left of the original six that had come there, and they sailed off to the stars. They came to Ozagen. And crashed. No wonder. The ship was so old."

"Is the wreck still around?"

"*Fi*. Close to where my sisters and aunts and cousins live."

"Your mother is dead?"

She hesitated, then nodded. "Yes. She died giving birth to me. And my sisters. My father died later. Or rather, we think he did. He went on a hunting party and never came back."

Hal frowned, and he said, "You told me that your mother and aunts were the last of the native human beings on Ozagen. That isn't so. Fobo told me that there are at least a thousand small isolated groups in the backlands. And you said once before that Rastignac was the only Earthman to get out alive from the wreck. He was your mother's husband, naturally . . . and incredible as it sounds, their union—one of a terrestrial and an extraterrestrial—was fertile! That alone would rock my colleagues on their heels. It's completely contrary to accepted science that thcir body chemistry and chromosomes should match! But—what I'm getting at is that your mother's sisters had children, too. If the last human male of your group died years before Rastignac crashed, who was their father?"

"My father, Jean-Jacques Rastignac. He was the husband of my mother and my three aunts. They all said that he was a superb lover, very experienced, very virile."

Hal said, "Oh."

Until she had the spaghetti and salad ready, he watched her in silence. By then he had regained some of his moral perspective. After all, the Frenchman was not too much worse than he himself was. Maybe not as bad. He chuckled. How easy it was to condemn somebody else for giving way to temptation until you yourself faced the same situation. He wondered what

Pornsen would have done if Jeannette had contacted him.

". . . and so, after we'd been going down that jungle river," she was saying, "they quit watching me so closely. We'd taken two months to get from my home, near where they'd captured me, so they thought I'd never dare to try to get home alone. There are too many deadly things in the jungle. They make the nightlifer look like a minor nuisance."

She shuddered.

"When we got to a village which was on the very edge of their civilization, they let me wander around in the enclosure. By then I'd learned some of their language and they some of mine. But our conversation was on a very simple level. One of their party, a scientist named 'Asa''atsi, put me through all sorts of examinations and tests, physical and mental. There was a machine at the village hospital which took photographs of my insides. My skeleton, my organs. *Maw tyuh!* My everything.

"They said it was most interesting. Imagine that! I am exposed as no woman has ever been exposed, and to them I am just most interesting. Indeed!"

"Well." Hal laughed. "You can't expect them to take the viewpoint of a male mammal toward a female mammal . . . that is . . ."

She looked archly at him. "And am I a mammal?"

"Obviously, unmistakably, indisputably, and enthusiastically."

"For that, you get a kiss."

She leaned over him and placed her mouth over his. He stiffened, reacting as he had when his ex-wife had offered to kiss him. But she must have anticipated this, for she said, "You are a man, not a pillar of stone. And I am a woman who loves you. Kiss me back; don't just take my kisses."

"Oh, not so hard," she murmured. "Kiss me. Don't try to ram your lips through mine. Go soft, melt, merge your lips with mine. See."

She vibrated the tip of her tongue against his. Then

she stood back, smiling, her eyes half-closed, her red lips wet. He was shaking and breathing hard.

"Do your people think the tongue is only to talk with? Do they think that what I did is wicked, unreal?"

"I don't know. Nobody ever discussed that."

"You liked it, I know. Yet this is the same mouth with which I eat. The one I must hide behind a veil when I sit across the table from you."

"Don't put the cap on," he blurted. "I have been thinking about that. There is no rational reason why we should be veiled when we eat. The only reason is that I have been taught it is disgusting. Pavlov's dog salivated when it heard the bell; I get sick when I see food go into a naked mouth."

"Let's eat. Then we will drink and we will talk of us. And later do whatever we feel like doing."

He was learning fast. He didn't even blush.

15

AFTER the meal she diluted a pitcher of beetle-juice with water, poured in a purplish liquid which made the drink smell like grapes, and dropped sprigs of an orange plant on the surface. Placed into a glass of ice cubes, it was cool and even tasted like grapes. It did not gag him at all.

"Why did you pick me instead of Pornsen?"

She sat on his lap, one arm around his neck, the other on the table, drink in hand.

"Oh, you were so good-looking, and he was so ugly. Besides, I could *feel* that you could be trusted. I knew I had to be careful. My father had told me about Earthmen. He said they couldn't be trusted."

"How true. But you must have an intuition for doing the right thing, Jeannette. If you had antennae, I'd say you could detect nervous emanations. Here, let's see!" He went to run his fingers through her hair, but she ducked her head and laughed.

He laughed with her and dropped his hand to her shoulder, rubbing the smooth skin. "I was probably the only person on the ship who wouldn't have betrayed you. But I'm in a quandary now. You see, your presence here raises the Backrunner. It puts me in grave danger—but a danger I wouldn't miss for anything else in the world.

"However, what you tell me of the X-ray machines

worries me. So far, we've seen none. Are the wogs hiding them? If so, why? We know that they have electricity, and that they're theoretically capable of inventing X-ray machines. Perhaps, they're hiding them only because they're indications of an even more developed technology.

"But that doesn't seem reasonable. And, after all, we don't know too much of Siddo culture. We've not been here long enough; we don't have enough men to do extensive investigation.

"Maybe I'm being too suspicious. That's more than likely. Nevertheless, Macneff should be informed. But I can't tell him how I found out; I wouldn't even dare make up a lie about my source of information.

"I'm on the horns of a dilemma."

"A dilemma? A beast I never heard of before."

He hugged her and said, "I hope you never do."

"Listen," she said, looking eagerly at him with her beautiful brown eyes, "why bother to tell Macneff? If the Siddo should attack the Haijac—or, as you say their enemies call them so aptly, Highjackers—and conquer them, why not? Couldn't we make our way to my homeland and live there?"

Hal was shocked. "Those are my people, my countrymen! They—we—are Sigmenites. I couldn't betray them!"

"You are doing just that now by keeping me here," she said gravely.

"I know that," said Hal slowly. "But it's not a gross betrayal, not a real betrayal at all. How am I hurting them by having you?"

"I don't worry at all about what you may be doing to them. I do worry about what you may be doing to yourself."

"To myself? I am doing the best thing I ever did!"

She laughed delightedly and gave him a light kiss on the lips.

But he frowned, and he said, "Jeannette, it's serious. Sooner or later, and probably sooner, we have to do something definite. By that, I mean find a hiding place deep underground. Later, after it's all over, we can come out. And we'll have at least eighty years to ourselves, which will be more than enough. Because it will take that long for the *Gabriel* to return to Earth and for the colonizing ships to come back. We'll be like Adam and Eve, just us two and the beasts."

"What do you mean?" she said, her eyes widening.

"This. Our specialists are working night and day on samples of blood the wogs gave us. They hope to make an artificial semivirus that will attach itself to the copper in the wog's blood cells and change the cells' electrophoretic properties."

"*'Ama?*"

"I'll try to explain even if I have to use a mixture of American, French, and Siddo to get it across.

"A form of this artificial semivirus is what killed most of Earth's people during the Apocalyptic War. I won't go into the historical details; it's enough to say that the virus was disseminated secretly from outside the Earth's atmosphere by the ships of Martian colonists. The descendants of Earthmen on Mars, who considered themselves true Martians, were led by Sigfried Russ, as evil a man as ever lived. Or so say the history books."

"I do not know what you are talking about," she said.

Her face was grave, her eyes fixed upon his face.

"You can pick up the gist of it. The four Martian ships, pretending to be merchant vessels orbiting before entry, dropped billions of these viruses. Invisible knots of protein molecules that drifted through the atmosphere, spreading throughout the world, covering it in a very tenuous mist. These molecules, once they penetrated a human being's skin, locked onto the hemoglobin in the red blood cells and gave them a positive charge. This charge caused one end of a globin molecule to bind with the end of the other. And the molecule would go into a kind of crystallization. This would twist the doughnut-shaped cells into scimitars and thus cause an artificial sickle-cell anemia.

"The lab-created anemia was much swifter and more certain than the natural anemia, because every blood cell in the body would be affected, not just a small percentage. Every cell would soon break down. No oxygen would be carried through the human organism; the body died.

"The body did die, Jeannette—the body of humanity. Almost an entire planet of human beings perished from lack of oxygen."

"I think I understand most of what you have told me," said Jeannette. "But everybody, they did not die?"

"No. And at the beginning, the governments of Earth found out what was going on. They launched missiles toward Mars; and the missiles, designed to cause earthquakes, destroyed most of the Martian underground colonies.

"On Earth, perhaps a million survived on each continent. With the exception of certain areas where almost the entire population was untouched. Why? We don't really know. But something, perhaps favorable wind currents, bent the fall of virus away until the virus had fallen to the ground. After a certain time outside of a human body, the virus died.

"Anyway, the islands of Hawaii and Iceland were left with organized governments and a full population. Israel, too, was left untouched, as if the hand of God had covered it during the deadly fall. And southern Australia and the Caucasus Mountains were spared.

"These groups spread out afterward, resettling the world, absorbing the survivors in the areas which they took over. In the jungles of Africa and the Malayan peninsula, enough were left alive to venture out. These reestablished themselves in their native lands before colonies from the islands and Australia could take over.

"And what happened to Earth is destined to happen here on this planet. When the order is given, missiles will leave the *Gabriel,* missiles laden with the same deadly cargo. Only, the viruses will be fitted for the blood cells of the Ozagen. And the missiles will circle and circle and drop their invisible rain of death. And . . . everywhere . . . the skulls—"

"Hush!" Jeannette put her finger on his quivering lips. "I don't know what you mean by proteins and molecules and those—those electrofrenetic charges! They're way above my head. But I do know that the longer you've been talking, the more scared you've been getting. Your voice was getting higher, and your eyes were growing wider.

"Somebody has frightened you in the past. No! Don't interrupt! They've scared you, and you've been man enough to hide most of your fear. But they've done such a horribly efficient job that you haven't been able to get over it.

"Well—" and she put her soft lips to his ear and whispered—"I'm going to wipe that fear out. I'm going to lead you out of that valley of fright. No! Don't protest! I know it hurts your ego to think that a woman could know you're afraid. But I don't think any the less of you. I admire you all the more because you've conquered so much of it. I know what courage it took to face the 'Meter. I know you did it because of me. I'm proud that you did. I love you for it. And I know what courage it takes to keep me here, when at any time a slip would send you to certain disgrace and death. I know what it all means. It's my nature and instinct and business and love to know.

"Now! Drink with me. We're not outside these walls where we have to worry ourselves about such things and be scared. We're in here. Away from everything except ourselves. Drink. And love me. I'll love you, Hal, and we'll not see the world outside nor need to. For the time being. Forget in my arms."

They kissed and ran their hands over each other and said the things lovers have always said.

Between kisses, Jeannette poured more of the purplish liquor, and they drank this. Hal had no trouble swallowing it. He decided that it wasn't the idea of drinking alcohol so much as it was the odor that sickened him. When his nose was deceived, his stomach was also. And every drink made it easier for the next one.

He downed three tall glasses and then rose and lifted Jeannette in his arms and carried her into the bedroom. She was kissing the side of his neck, and it seemed to him that an electric charge was passing from her lips to his skin and on up to his brain and on down through his beating chest and warming stomach and swelling genital and on down through the soles of his feet, which, strangely, had become ice. Certainly, holding her did not make him want to withdraw as when he had carried out his duty toward Mary and the Sturch.

Yet, even in his ecstasy of anticipation, there was a stronghold of retreat. It was small, but it was there, dark in the middle of the fire. He could not completely forget himself, and he doubted, wondering if he would fail as he had sometimes when he had crawled into bed in the dark and reached out for Mary.

There was also a black seed of panic, dropped by the doubt. If he failed, he would kill himself. He would be done forever.

Yet, he told himself, it could not possibly happen, must not. Not when he had his arms around her and her lips were on his.

He put her on the bed and then turned off the ceiling light. But she turned on the lamp over the bed.

"Why are you doing *that?*" he said, standing at the foot of the bed, feeling the rise of panic and the fall of his passion. At the same time he wondered how she could so swiftly, unseen by him, have unclothed herself.

She smiled and said, "Remember what you told me the other day? That beautiful passage: *God said, Let there be light.*"

"We do not need it."

"I do. I must see you at every moment. The dark

would take away half of the pleasure. I want to see you in love."

She reached upward to adjust the angle of the bed-lamp, her breasts rising with the movement and sending an almost intolerable pang through him.

"There. Now I can see your face. Especially, at the moment when I will know best that you love me."

She extended a foot and touched his knee with her toe. Skin upon skin . . . it drew him forward as if it were the finger of an angel gently directing him toward destiny. He knelt upon the bed, and she drew back her leg with her toe still placed upon his leg as if it had grown roots into his flesh and could not be dislodged.

"Hal, Hal," she murmured. "What have they done to you? What have they done to all your men? I know from what you have told me that they are like you. What have they done? Made you hate instead of love, though they call hate love. Made you half-men so you will turn your drive into yourself and then outward against the enemy. So you will become fierce warriors because you are such timid lovers."

"That's not true," he said. "Not true."

"I can see you. It is true."

She removed her foot and placed it beside his knee and said, "Come closer," and when he had moved closer, still on his knees, she reached up and pulled him down against her breasts.

"Place your mouth here. Become a baby again. And I will raise you so you forget your hate and know only love. And become a man."

"Jeannette, Jeannette," he said hoarsely. He put out his hand to pull the cord of the bedlamp and said, "Not the light."

But she put her hand on his and said, "Yes, the light."

Then she took her hand away and said, "All right, Hal. Turn it off. For a little while. If you must go back into the darkness, go far back. Far back. And then be reborn . . . for a little while. Then, the light."

"No! Let it stay on!" he snarled. "I am not in my

mother's womb. I do not want to go back there; I do not need to. And I will take you as an army takes a city."

"Don't be a soldier, Hal. Be a lover. You must love me, not rape me. You can't take me, because I will surround you."

Her hand closed gently on him, and she arched her back slightly, and suddenly he was surrounded. A shock ran through him, comparable to that he had felt when she kissed his neck, but comparable only in kind and not in intensity.

He started to bury his face against her shoulder, but she put both hands on his chest and with surprising strength, half-raised him.

"No. I must see your face. Especially at *the time* I must, for I want to see you lose yourself in me."

And she kept her eyes wide open throughout as if she were trying to impress forever upon every cell of her body her lover's face.

Hal was not disconcerted, for he would not have paid attention to the Archurielite himself knocking on the door. But he noticed, though he did not think of it, that the pupils of her eyes had contracted to a pencil point.

16

THE alcoholics in the Haijac Union were sent to H. Therefore, no psychological or narcotic therapies had been worked out for addicts. Hal, frustrated by this fact in his desire to wipe out Jeannette's weakness, went for medicine to the very people who had given her the disease. But he pretended that the cure was for himself.

Fobo said, "There is widespread drinking on Ozagen, but it is light. Our few alcoholics are empathized into normality with the help of medicine, of course. Why don't you let me empathize you?"

"Sorry. My government forbids that."

He had given Fobo the same excuse for not inviting the wog into his apartment.

"You have the most forbidding government," said Fobo and went into one of his long, howling laughs.

When he recovered, he said, "You're forbidden to touch liquor, too, but that doesn't hold you back. Well, there's no accounting for inconsistency. Seriously, though, I have just the thing for you. It's called Easyglow. We put it into the daily ration of liquor, slowly increasing the Easyglow and diminishing the alcohol. In two or three weeks, the patient is drinking from a fluid ninety-six percent Easyglow. The taste is much the same; the drinker seldom suspects. Continued treatment eases the patient from his dependence on the alcohol. There is only one drawback."

He paused and said, "The drinker is now addicted to Easyglow!"

He whooped and slapped his thigh and shook his head until his long cartilaginous nose vibrated, and laughed until the tears came.

When he managed to quit laughing and had dried his tears with a starfish-shaped handkerchief, he said, "Really, the peculiar effect of Easyglow is that it opens the patient for discharge of the strains that have driven him to drink. He may then be empathized and at the same time weaned from the stimulant. Since I have no opportunity to slip the stuff to you secretly, I'm taking the chance that you are seriously interested in curing yourself. When you're ready for therapy, tell me."

Hal took the bottle to his apartment. Every day, its contents went quietly and carefully into the beetlejuice he got for Jeannette. He hoped that he was psychologist enough to cure her once the Easyglow took effect.

Although he didn't know it, he was himself being "cured" by Fobo. His almost daily talks with the empathist instilled doubts about the religion and science of the Haijacs. Fobo read the biographies of Isaac Sigmen and the *Works:* the *Pre-Torah, The Western Talmud,* the *Revised Scriptures,* the *Foundations of Serialism, Time and Theology, The Self and the World Line.* Calmly sitting at his table with a glass of juice in his hand, the wog challenged the mathematics of the dunnologists. Hal proved; Fobo disproved. He pointed out that the mathematics was based mainly on false-to-fact assumptions; that Dunne's and Sigmen's reasoning was buttressed by too many false analogies, metaphors, and strained interpretations. Remove the buttresses, and the structure fell.

"Moreover and to continue," Fobo said, "allow and permit me to point out one more in a score of contradictions embodied in your theology. You Sigmenites believe that every person is responsible for any event happening to him, that no one else but the self may be blamed. If you, Hal Yarrow, stumbled on a toy left by some careless child—happy, happy infant with no responsibilities!—and skinned your elbow, you did so because you really wanted to hurt yourself. If you are seriously hurt in an 'accident,' it was no accident; it was you agreeing to actualize a potentiality. Contrarily, you could have agreed with your self not to be involved, and so actualized a different future.

"If you commit a crime, you wish to do so. If you get caught, it is not because you were stupid in the commission of the crime or because the Uzzites were more clever or because circumstances worked out to make you fall into the hands of—what is your vernacular for them, the uzz? No, it was because you wished to be caught; you, somehow, controlled the circumstances.

"If you die, it is because you wanted to die, not because someone pointed a gun at you and pulled the trigger. You died because you willed to intercept the bullet; you agreed with the killer that you could be killed.

"Of course, this philosophy, this belief, is very *shib* for the Sturch, for it relieves them of any blame if they have to chastise or execute or unjustly tax you or in any way take uncivil liberties with you. Obviously, if you did not wish to be chastised or executed or taxed or dealt with in an unfair way, you would not permit it.

"Of course, if you do disagree with the Sturch or try to defy it, you do so because you are trying to realize a pseudofuture, one condemned by the Sturch. You, the individual, can't win.

"Yet, hear and listen to this: You also believe that you yourself have perfect free will to determine the future. But the future has been determined because Sigmen has gone ahead in time and arranged it. Sigmen's brother, Jude Changer, may temporarily disarrange the future and the past, but Sigmen will eventually restore the desired equilibrium.

"Let me ask and question you, how can you yourself determine the future when the future has been determined and forecast by Sigmen? One state or the other may be correct, but not both."

"Well," Hal said, his face hot, his chest feeling as if a heavy weight were on it, his hands shaking, "I have thought of that very question."

"Did you ask anyone?"

"No," Hal said, feeling trapped. "We were allowed to ask questions, of course, of our teachers. But that question was not on the list."

"You mean to tell me that your questions were written out for you and you were confined to those?"

"Well, why not?" Hal said angrily. "Those questions were for our benefit. The Sturch knew from long experience what questions students ask, so it listed them for the less bright."

"Less bright is right," said Fobo. "And I suppose that any questions not on the list were considered too dangerous, too conducive to unrealistic thinking?"

Hal nodded miserably.

Fobo went on in his relentless dissection. Worse, far worse than anything he had said were his next words, for they were a personal attack on the sacrosanct self of Sigmen himself.

He said that the Forerunner's biographies and theological writings revealed him to an objective reader as a sexually frigid and woman-hating man with a Messiah complex and paranoid and schizophrenic tendencies which burst through his icy shell from time to time in religious-scientific frenzies and fantasies.

"Other men," Fobo said, "must have stamped their personalities and ideas upon their times. But Sigmen had an advantage over those great leaders who came before him. Because of Earth's rejuvenation serums, he lived long enough, not only to set up his kind of society, but also to consolidate it and weed out its weaknesses. He didn't die until the cement of his social form had hardened."

"But the Forerunner didn't die," Yarrow protested. "He left in time. He is still with us, traveling down the fields of presentation, skipping here and there, now to the past, now to the future. Always, wherever he is needed to turn pseudotime into real time, he is there."

"Ah, yes," Fobo smiled. "That was the reason you went to the ruins, was it not? To check up on a mural which hinted that the Ozagen humans had once been visited by a man from another star? You thought it might have been the Forerunner, didn't you?"

"I still think so," said Hal. "But my report showed that though the man resembled Sigmen somewhat, the evidence was too inconclusive. The Forerunner may or may not have visited this planet a thousand years ago."

"Be that as it may, I maintain your theses are meaningless. You claim that his prophecies came true. I say, first, that they were ambiguously stated. Second, if they have been realized it is because your powerful state-church—which you economically term the Sturch —has made strenuous efforts to fulfill them.

"Furthermore, this pyramidal society of yours—this guardian-angel administration—where every twenty-five families have a *gapt* to supervise their most intimate and minute details, and every twenty-five family-*gapts* have a block-*gapt* at their head, and every fifty block-*gapts* are directed by a supervisor-*gapt,* and so on—this society is based on fear and ignorance and suppression."

Hal, shaken, angered, shocked, would get up to leave. Fobo would call him back and ask him to disprove what he'd said. Hal would let loose a flood of wrath. Sometimes, when he had finished, he would be asked to sit down and continue the discussion. Sometimes, Fobo would lose his temper; they would shout and scream insults. Twice, they fought with fists; Hal got a bloody nose, and Fobo a black eye. Then the wog, weeping, would embrace Hal and ask for his forgiveness, and they would sit down and drink some more until their nerves were calmed.

Hal knew that he should not listen to Fobo, should not allow himself to be in a situation where he could hear such unrealism. But he could not stay away. And, though he hated Fobo for what he said, he derived a strange satisfaction and fascination from the relationship. He could not cut himself off from this being whose tongue cut and flayed him far more painfully than Pornsen's whip ever had.

He told Jeannette of these incidents. She encouraged him to tell them over and over again until he had talked away the stress and strain of grief and hate and doubt. Afterward, there was always love such as he had never thought possible. For the first time, he knew that man and woman could become one flesh. His wife and he had remained outside the circle of each other, but Jeannette knew the geometry that would take him in and the chemistry that would mix his substance with hers.

Always, too, there was the light and the drink. But they did not bother him. Unknown to her, she was now drinking a liquor almost entirely Easyglow. And he had gotten used to the light above their bed. It was one of her quirks. Fear of the dark wasn't behind it, because it was only while making love that she required that the lamp be left on. He didn't understand it. Perhaps she wanted to impress his image on her memory, always to have it if she ever lost him. If so, let her keep the light.

By its glow he explored her body with an interest that was part sexual and part anthropological. He was delighted and astonished at the many small differences between her and Terran women. There was a small appendage of skin on the roof of her mouth that might have been the rudiment of some organ whose function had been long ago cast aside by evolution. She had twenty-eight teeth; the wisdom teeth were missing. That might or might not have been a characteristic of her mother's people.

He suspected that she had either an extra set of pectoral muscles or else an extraordinarily well developed normal set. Her large and cone-shaped breasts did not sag. They were high and firm and pointed slightly upward: the ideal of feminine beauty so often portrayed through the ages by male sculptors and painters and so seldom existing in nature.

She was not only a pleasure to look at; she was pleasing to be with. At least once a week she would greet him with a new garment. She loved to sew; out of the materials he gave her she fashioned blouses, skirts, and even gowns. Along with the change in dress went new hairdos. She was ever new and ever beautiful, and she made him realize for the first time that a woman could be beautiful. Or perhaps she made him realize that a human being could be beautiful. And a thing of beauty was a joy, if not forever, then for a long time.

His enjoyment of her, and hers of him, was hastened and strengthened by her linguistic fluency. She seemed to have switched from her French to American almost overnight. Within a week she was speaking, within her limited but quickly increasing vocabulary, faster and more expressively than he.

However, his delight in her company made him neglect his duties. His progress in learning to read Siddo slowed down.

One day, Fobo asked him how he was doing with the books he'd loaned him. Hal confessed that they were too difficult for him—so far. Fobo then gave him a book on evolution which was used in the wog elementary schools.

"Try these. They're two volumes, but they're rather slim in text. The many pictures will enable you to grasp the text more quickly. It's an abridgement for the youngsters by a famous educator, We'enai."

Jeannette had much more time to study than Hal, since she had little to do in the apartment while he was gone during the day. She tackled the new books, and so Hal fell into the lazy habit of allowing her to translate for him. She would first read the Siddo aloud and then translate into American. Or, if her vocabulary failed her, into French.

One evening, she started out energetically enough. But she was sipping beetlejuice between paragraphs, and after a while she began to lose interest in the translating.

She went through the first chapter, which described the formation of the planet and the beginnings of life. In the second chapter, she yawned quite openly and looked at Hal, but he closed his eyes and pretended not to notice. So she read of the rise of the wogs from a prearthropod that had changed its mind and decided to become a chordate. We'enai made some heavy jests about the contrariness of the wogglebugs since that fateful day, and then took up, in the third chapter, the story of mammalian evolution on the other large continent of Ozagen which climaxed in man.

She quoted, " 'But man, like us, had its mimical parasites. One was a different species of the so-called tavern beetle. It, instead of resembling a wog, looked like a man. Like its counterpart, it could fool no intelligent person, but its gift of alcohol made it very acceptable to man. It, too, accompanied its host from primitive times, became an integral part of his civilization, and, finally, according to one theory, a large cause of man's downfall.

" 'Humanity's disappearance from the face of Ozagen is due not only to the tavern beetle, if it was at all. That creature can be controlled. Like most things, it can be abused or its purpose distorted so that it becomes a menace.

" 'This is what man did with it.

" 'He had, it must be noted, an ally to help him in the misuse of the insect. This was another parasite, one of a somewhat different kind; one that was, indeed, our cousin, in a manner speaking.

" 'One thing, however, distinguishes it from us, and from man, and from any other animal on this planet with the exception of some very low species. That is, that from the very first fossil evidence we have of it, it was wholly—' "

Jeannette put the book down. "I don't know the next word. Hal, do I have to read this? It's so boring."

"No. Forget it. Read me one of those comics that you and the *Gabriel*'s sailors like so much."

She smiled, a beautiful sight, and she began reading Volume 1037, Book 56, *The Adventures of Leif Magnus, Beloved Disciple of the Forerunner, When He Met the Horror from Arcturus.*

He listened to her efforts to translate the American into the vernacular wog until he grew tired of the banalities of the comic and pulled her down to him.

Always, there was the light left on above them.

Yet, they had their misunderstandings, their disagreements, their conflicts.

Jeannette was neither puppet nor slave. When she did not like something Hal did or said, she was often quick to say so. And, if he replied sarcastically or violently, he was likely to find himself attacked verbally.

Not too long after he had hidden Jeannette in his *puka,* he returned after a long day at the ship with a heavy growth of stubble on his face.

Jeannette, after kissing him, made a face and said, "That hurts; it is like a file. I'll get your cream and rub off your whiskers myself."

"No, don't do that," he said.

"Why not?" she said as she walked toward the unmentionable. "I love to do things for you. And I especially love to make you look nice."

She returned with the can of depilatory in her hand.

"Now, you sit down, and I will do all your work for you. You can think of how much I love you while I'm removing those so-scratchy wires on your face."

"You don't understand, Jeannette. I can't shave. I am a *lamedhian* now, and *lamedhians* must wear beards."

She stopped walking toward him and said, "You *must?* You mean that it is the law, that you will be a criminal if you don't?"

"No, not exactly," he said. "The Forerunner himself never said a word about it, nor has any law been passed making it compulsory. But—it is the custom.

And it is a sign of honor, for only a man worthy to wear a *lamedh* is allowed to grow a beard."

"What would happen if a non-*lamedhian* grew one?"

"I don't know," he said, annoyance apparent in his voice. "It has never happened. It's—just one of those things you take for granted. Something only an outsider would think about."

"But a beard is so ugly," she said. "And it scratches my face. I would as soon kiss a pile of bedsprings."

"Then," he said angrily, "you'll either have to learn to kiss bedsprings or learn to get along without kisses. Because I *have* to have a beard!"

"Listen to me," she said, going up close to him. "You don't *have* to! What is the use of being a *lamedhian* if you don't have any more freedom than before, if you must do what is expected of you? Why can't you just ignore the custom?"

Hal began to feel both fury and panic. Panic because he might alienate her so far she would leave and because he knew that if he gave in to her he would be regarded suspiciously by the other *lamedhians* on the *Gabriel*.

As a result, he accused her of being a stupid fool. She replied with equal heat and harshness. They quarreled; the night was half over before she made the first movement toward a reconciliation. Then, it was dawn before they were through proving they loved each other.

In the morning, he shaved. Nothing happened at the *Gabriel* for three days, nobody made any remarks, and he put down to guilt and imagination the strange looks he saw—or thought he saw. Finally, he began to think that either nobody had noticed or else they were so busy with their duties that they did not think it worthwhile to comment. He even began wondering if there were other annoyances connected with being a *lamedhian* which he could do away with.

Then, the morning of the fourth day, he was called to the office of Macneff.

He found the Sandalphon sitting behind his desk and fingering his own beard. Macneff stared with his pale blue eyes at Hal for some time before replying to Hal's greeting.

"Perhaps, Yarrow," he said, "you have been too concerned with your researches among the wogs to think about other things. It is true we live in an abnormal environment here, and we are all concentrating on the day we start the project."

He rose and began pacing back and forth before Hal.

"You surely must know that as a *lamedhian,* you not only have privileges, you have responsibilities?"

"*Shib, abba.*"

Macneff suddenly wheeled on Hal and pointed a long bony finger at him.

"Then, why aren't you growing a beard?" he said loudly. And he glared.

Hal felt himself grow cold, as he had so often when he was a child and his *gapt,* Pornsen, had made this same maneuver toward him. And he felt the same mental confusion.

"Why, I—I—"

"We must strive not only to attain the *lamedh,* we must strive to continue to be worthy of it. Purity and purity alone will make us succeed, unending effort to be pure!"

"Your pardon, *abba,*" said Hal, his voice quivering. "But I am making a never-ending effort to be pure."

He dared to look the Sandalphon in the eyes when he said that, though where he got the courage he did not know. To lie so outrageously, he who was living in unreality, to lie in the presence of the great and pure Sandalphon!

"However," Hal continued, "I did not know that shaving would have anything to do with my purity. There is nothing in *The Western Talmud* or any of the Forerunner's books about the reality or unreality of a beard."

"Are you telling me what is in the scriptures?" shouted Macneff.

"No, of course not. But, what I said is true, isn't it?"

Macneff resumed his pacing, and he said, "We must be pure, must be pure. And even the slightest hint of pseudofuture, the smallest departure from reality, may dirty us. Yes, Sigmen never said anything about this. But it has long been recognized that only the pure are worthy to emulate the Forerunner by having a beard. Therefore, to be pure, we must look pure."

"I agree with you wholeheartedly," said Hal.

He was beginning to find courage in himself, a firmness. It had suddenly occurred to him that he felt so shaken because he was reacting to Macneff as he had to Pornsen. But Pornsen was dead, defeated, his ashes thrown to the wind. And it had been Hal himself who had scattered them at the ceremony.

"Under ordinary circumstances, I would let my whiskers grow," he said. "But I am living among the wogs now so I may do more effective espionage, besides conducting my researches. And I have found out that the wogs regard a beard as an abomination; they have no beards themselves, you know. They do not understand why we let ours grow if we have means to remove them. And they feel uneasy and disgusted when in the presence of a bearded man. I can't gain their confidence if I have one.

"However, I plan to grow one the moment the project is begun."

"Hmm!" said Macneff, fingering the hairs on his face. "You may have something there. After all, these are unusual circumstances. But why didn't you tell me?"

"You are so busy, from morning to bedtime, that I did not want to bother you," said Hal. He was wondering if Macneff would take the time and trouble to investigate the truth of his statement. For the wogs had never said one word to Hal about beards. He had been inspired to make his excuse when he remembered having read about the initial reactions of the American Indians to the facial growth of white men.

Macneff, after a few more words on the importance of keeping pure, dismissed Hal.

And Hal, shaking from the reaction of the lecture, went home. There, he had a few drinks to calm himself, then a few more to uninhibit himself for the supper with Jeannette. He had discovered that if he drank enough, he could overcome the disgust he felt on seeing food go into her naked mouth.

17 ✕

ONE day, Yarrow, returning from the market with a large box, said, "You've really been putting away the groceries lately. You're not eating for two? Or maybe three?"

She paled. *"Maw choo!* Do you know what you're saying?"

He put the box on a table and grabbed her shoulders.

"Shib. I do. Jeannette, I've been thinking about that very thing for a long time, but I haven't said anything. I didn't want to worry you. Tell me, are you?"

She looked him straight in the eye, but her body was shaking. "Oh, no. It is impossible!"

"Why should it be?"

"Fi. But I know—don't ask me how—that it cannot be. But you must never say things like that. Not even joking. I can't stand it."

He pulled her close and said over her shoulder, "Is it because you can't? Because you know you'll never bear my children?"

Her thick, faintly perfumed hair nodded.

"I know. Don't ask me how I know."

He held her at arm's length again.

"Listen, Jeannette. I'll tell you what's been troubling you. You and I are of different species. Your mother and father were, too. Yet they had children. However, you may know that the ass and the mare have young, too, but the mule is sterile. The lion and the tigress may breed, but the liger or tigon can't. Isn't that right? You're afraid you're a mule!"

She put her head on his chest; tears fell on his shirt.

He said, "Let's be real about this, honey. Maybe you are. So what? Forerunner knows that our situation is bad enough without a baby to complicate it. We'll be lucky if you are . . . uh . . . well, we have each other, haven't we? That's all I want. You."

He couldn't keep from being reflective as he dried her tears and kissed her and helped her put the food in the refrigerator.

The quantities of groceries and milk she had been consuming were more than a normal amount, especially the milk. There had been no telltale change in her superb figure. She could not eat that much without some kind of effect. A month passed. He watched her closely. She ate enormously. Nothing happened.

Yarrow put it down to his ignorance of her alien metabolism.

Another month. Hal was just leaving the ship's library when Turnboy, the historian *joat,* stopped him.

"The rumor is that the techs have finally made the globin-locking molecule," the historian said. "I think that this time the grapevine's right. A conference is called for fifteen hundred."

"Shib."

Hal kept his despair out of his voice.

When the meeting broke up at 1650, it left him with sagging shoulders. The virus was already in production. In a week, a large enough supply would be made to fill the disseminators of six prowler torpedoes. The plan was to release them to wipe out the city of Siddo. The prowlers would fly in spirals whose range would expand until a large territory was covered. Eventually, as the prowlers returned for reloading and then went out again, the entire planet of wogs would be slain.

When he got home, he found Jeannette lying in

bed, her hair a black corona on the pillow. She smiled
weakly.

He forgot his mood in a thrill of concern.

"What's the matter, Jeannette?"

He laid his hand on her forehead. The skin was
dry, hot, and rough.

"I don't know. I haven't been feeling really well for
two weeks, but I didn't complain. I thought I'd get
over it. Today, I felt so bad I just had to go back to
bed after breakfast."

"We'll get you well."

He sounded confident. Inside himself, he was lost.
If she had contracted a serious disease, she could get
no doctor, no medicine.

For the next few days she continued to lie in bed.
Her temperature fluctuated from 99.5 in the morning
to 100.2 at night. Hal attended her as ably as he
could. He put wet towels and ice bags on her head and
gave her aspirin. She had stopped eating so much food;
all she wanted was liquid. She was always asking for
milk. Even the beetlejuice and the cigarettes were
turned down.

Her illness was bad enough, but her silences stung
Yarrow into a frenzy. As long as he had known her,
she had chattered lightly, merrily, amusingly. She could
be quiet, but it was with an interested wordlessness.
Now she let him talk; and when he quit, she did not
fill his silence with questions or comments.

In an effort to arouse her, he told her of his plan
to steal a gig and take her back to her jungle home.
A light came into her dulled eyes; the brown looked
shiny for the first time. She even sat up while he put
a map of the continent on her lap. She indicated the
general area where she had lived, and then she described the mountain range that rose from the jungle
and the tableland on its top where her aunts and sisters
lived in the ruins of an ancient metropolis.

Hal sat down at the little hexagon-shaped tabletop
by the bed and worked out the coordinates from the
maps. Now and then, he glanced up. She was lying

on her side, her white and delicate shoulder rising from her nightgown, her eyes large in the shadows around them.

"All I have to do is steal a little key," he said. "You see, the meter gauge on a gig is set at zero before every flight from the field. The boat will run fifty kilometers on manual. But, once the tape passes fifty, the gig automatically stops and sends out a location signal. That's to keep anybody from running away. However, the autos can be unlocked and the signal turned off. A little key will do it. I can get it. Don't worry."

"You must love me very much."

"You're *shib* as *shib* I do!"

He rose and kissed her. Her mouth, once so soft and dewy, felt dry and hard. It was almost as if the skin were turning to horn.

He returned to his calculations. An hour later, a sigh from her made him look up. Her eyes were closed and her lips were slightly open. Sweat ran down her face.

He hoped her fever had broken. No. The mercury had risen to 100.3.

She said something.

He bent down.

"What?"

She was muttering in an unknown language, the speech of her mother's people. Delirious.

Hal swore. He had to act. No matter what the consequences. He ran into the bathroom, shook from a bottle a ten-grain rockabye tablet, returned, and propped Jeannette up. With difficulty he managed to get her to wash the pill down with a glass of water.

After he locked her bedroom door, he put on a hood and cloak and walked fast to the nearest wog pharmacy. There he purchased three 20-gauge needles, three syringes, and some anti-coagulant. Back in his apartment, he tried to insert the needle in her arm vein. The point refused to go in until the fourth attempt when, in a fit of exasperation, he pressed hard.

During none of the jabbings did she open her eyes or jerk her arm.

When the first fluid crept into the glass tube, he gasped with relief. Though he hadn't known it, he had been biting his lip and holding his breath. Suddenly, he knew that he had for the last month been pushing a horrible suspicion back to the outlands of his mind. Now, he realized the thought had been ridiculous.

The blood was red.

He tried to arouse her in order to get a specimen of urine. She twisted her mouth over strange syllables, then lapsed back into sleep or a coma—he didn't know which. In an anguish of despair, he slapped her face, again and again, hoping he could bring her to. He swore once more, for he realized all at once that he should have gotten the specimen before giving her the rockabye. How stupid could he get! He wasn't thinking straight; he was too excited over her condition and what he had to do at the ship.

He made some very strong coffee and managed to get part of it down her. The rest dribbled down her chin and soaked her gown.

Either the caffeine or his desperate tone awoke her, for she opened her eyes long enough to look at him while he explained what he wanted her to do and where he was going afterward. After he had gotten the urine into a previously boiled jar, he wrapped the syringes and jar in a handkerchief and dropped them into the cloak pocket.

He had wristphoned the *Gabriel* for a gig. A horn beeped outside. He took another look at Jeannette, locked the bedroom door, and ran down the stairs. The gig hovered above the curb. He entered, sat down, and punched the GO button. The boat rose to a thousand feet and then flashed at an 11-degree angle toward the park where the ship squatted.

The medical section was empty, except for one orderly. The fellow dropped his comic and jumped to his feet.

"Take it easy," said Hal. "I just want to use the

Labtech. And I don't want to be bothered with making out triplicate forms. This is a little personal matter, see?"

Hal had taken off his cloak, so the orderly could see the bright golden *lamedh.*

"*Shib,*" the orderly grunted.

Hal gave him two cigarettes.

"Geez, thanks." The orderly lit a cigarette, sat down, and picked up *The Forerunner and Delilah in the Wicked City of Gaza.*

Yarrow went around the corner of the Labtech, where the orderly couldn't see him, and set the proper dials. After he inserted his specimens, he sat down. Within a few seconds, he jumped up and began pacing back and forth. Meanwhile, the huge cube of the Labtech purred like a contented cat as it digested its strange food. A half-hour later, it rumbled once and then flashed a green light: ANALYSIS COMPLETE.

Hal pressed a button. Like a tongue out of a metal mouth, a long tape slid out. He read the code. Urine was normal. No infection there. Also normal were the pH and the blood count.

He hadn't been sure the "eye" would recognize the cells in her blood. However, the chances had been strong that her red cells would be Terranlike. Why not? Evolution, even on planets separated by light-years, follows parallel paths; the biconcave disk is the most efficient form for carrying the maximum of oxygen.

Or at least he'd thought so until he'd seen the corpuscles of an Ozagenian.

The machine chattered. More tape. Unknown hormone! Similar in molecular structure to the parathyroid hormone primarily concerned in the control of calcium metabolism.

What did that mean? Could the mysterious substance loosed in her bloodstream be the cause of her trouble?

More clicks. The calcium content of the blood was 40 milligram percent.

Strange. Such an abnormally high percentage should mean that the renal threshold was passed and that an excess of calcium should be "spilling" into the urine. Where was it going?

The Labtech flashed a red light: FINISHED.

He took a hematology textbook down from the shelf and opened it to the Ca section. When he quit reading, he straightened his shoulders. New hope? Perhaps. Her case sounded as if she had a form of hypercalcemia, which was manifested by any number of diseases ranging from rickets and steomalacia to chronic hypertrophic arthritis. Whatever she had, she was suffering from a malfunction of the parathyroid glands.

The next move was to the Pharm machine. He punched three buttons, dialed a number, waited for two minutes, and then lifted a little door at waist level. A tray slid out. On it was a cellophane sheath containing a hypodermic needle and a tube holding 30 cubic centimeters of a pale blue fluid. It was Jesper's serum, a "one-shot" readjustor of the parathyroid.

Hal put on his cloak, stuck the package in the inside pocket, and strode out. The orderly didn't even look up.

The next step was the weapons room. There he gave the storekeeper an order—made out in triplicate —for one 1 mm. automatic and a clip of one hundred explosive cartridges. The keeper only glanced over the forged signatures—he, too, was awed by the *lamedh*— and unlocked the door. Hal took the gun, which he could easily hide in the palm of his hand, and stuck it in his pants pocket.

At the key room, two corridors away, he repeated the crime. Or rather, he tried to.

Moto, the officer on duty, looked at the papers, hesitated, and said, "I'm sorry. My orders are to check on any requests with the Chief Uzzite. That won't be possible for about an hour, though. He's in conference with the Archurielite."

Hal picked up his papers.

"Never mind. My business'll hold. Be back in the morning."

On the way home, he planned what he would do. After injecting Jesper's serum into Jeannette, he would move her into the gig. The floor beneath the gig's control panel would have to be ripped up, two wires would be unhooked, and one connected to another lead. That would remove the fifty-mile limit. Unfortunately, it would also set off an alarm back in the *Gabriel*.

He hoped that he could take off straight up, level off, and dive behind the range of hills to the west of Siddo. The hills would deflect the radar. The autopilot could be set long enough for him to demolish the box that would be sending out the signal by which the *Gabriel* might track him down.

After that, with the gig hedgehopping, he could hope to be free until daybreak. Then, he'd submerge in the nearest lake or river deep enough until nightfall. During the darkness, he could rise and speed toward the tropics. If his radar showed any signs of pursuit, he could plunge again into a body of water. Fortunately, there was no sonar equipment on the *Gabriel*.

He left the long needle-shaped gig parked by the curb. His feet pounded the stairs. The key missed the hole the first two tries. He slammed the door without bothering to lock it again.

"Jeannette!"

Suddenly, he was afraid that she might have gotten up while delirious and somehow opened the doors and wandered out.

A low moan answered him. He unlocked the bedroom door and shoved it open. She was lying with her eyes wide.

"Jeannette. Do you feel better?"

"No. Worse. Much worse."

"Don't worry, baby. I've got just the medicine that'll put new life in you. In a couple of hours you'll be sitting up and yelling for steaks. And you won't even want to touch that milk. You'll be drinking your Easyglow by the gallon. And then—"

He faltered as he saw her face. It was a stony mask of distress, like the grotesque and twisted wooden masks of the Greek tragedians.

"Oh, no . . . *no!*" she moaned. "What did you say? Easyglow?" Her voice rose. "Is *that* what you've been giving me?"

"*Shib,* Jeannette. Take it easy. You liked it. What's the difference? The point is that we're going—"

"Oh, Hal, Hal! What have you done?"

Her pitiful face tore at him. Tears were falling; if ever a stone could weep, it was weeping now.

He turned and ran into the kitchen where he took out the sheath, removed the contents, and inserted the needle in the tube. He went back into the bedroom. She said nothing as he thrust the point into her vein. For a moment, he was afraid the needle would break. The skin was almost brittle.

"This stuff cures Earthpeople in a jiffy," he said, with what he hoped was a cheery bedside manner.

"Oh, Hal, come here. It's—it's too late now."

He withdrew the needle, rubbed alcohol on the break, and put a pad on it. Then he dropped to his knees by the bed and kissed her. Her lips were leathery.

"Hal, do you love me?"

"Won't you ever believe me? How many times must I tell you?"

"No matter what you'll find out about me?"

"I know all about you."

"No, you don't. You can't. Oh, Great Mother, if only I'd told you! Maybe you'd have loved me just as much, anyway. Maybe—"

"Jeannette! What's the matter?"

Her lids had closed. Her body shook in a spasm. When the violent trembling passed, she whispered with stiff lips. He bent his head to hear her.

"What did you say? Jeannette! Speak!"

He shook her. The fever must have died, for her shoulder was cold. And hard.

The words came low and slurring.

"Take me to my aunts and sisters. They'll know what to do. Not for me . . . but for the—"

"What do you mean?"

"Hal, will you always love—"

"Yes, yes. You know that! We've got more important things to do than talk about that."

If she heard him, she gave no sign. Her head was tilted far back with her exquisite nose pointed at the ceiling. Her lids and mouth were closed, and her hands were by her side, palms up. The breasts were motionless. Whatever breath she might have was too feeble to stir them.

18

Hal pounded on Fobo's door until it opened.

The empathist's wife said, "Hal, you startled me!"

"Where's Fobo?"

"He's at a college board meeting."

"I've got to see him at once."

Abasa yelled after him, "If it's important, go ahead! Those meetings bore him, anyway!"

By the time Yarrow had taken the steps three at a time and beelined across the nearby campus, his lungs were on fire. He didn't slacken his pace; he hurtled up the steps of the administration building and burst into the board room.

When he tried to speak, he had to stop and suck in deep breaths.

Fobo jumped out of his chair.

"What's up?"

"You—you've—got to come. Matter—life—death!"

"Excuse me, gentlemen," Fobo said.

The ten wogs nodded their heads and resumed the conference. The empathist put on his cloak and skullcap with its artificial antennae and led Hal out.

"Now, what is it?"

"Listen. I've got to trust you. I know you can't promise me anything. But I think you won't turn me in to my people. You're a real person, Fobo."

"Get to the point, my friend."

"Listen. You wogs are as advanced as we in endocrinology, even if you lag way behind in other sciences. And you've got an advantage. You have made some medical examinations and tests on her. You should know something about her anatomy and physiology and metabolism. You—"

"Jeannette? Oh, Jeannette Rastignac! The *lalitha!*"

"Yes. I've been hiding her in my apartment."

"I know."

"You know? But how? I mean—"

The wog put his hand on Hal's shoulder.

"There's something you should know. I meant to tell you tonight after I got home. This morning a man named Art Hunah Pukui rented an apartment in a building across the street. He claimed he wanted to live among us so he could learn our language and our mores more swiftly.

"But he's spent most of his time in this building carrying around a case which I imagine contains various devices to enable him to hear from a distance the sounds in your apartment. However, the landlord kept an eye on him, so he wasn't able to plant any of his devices."

"Pukui is an Uzzite."

"If you say so. Right now he's in his apartment watching this building through a powerful telescope."

"And he could be listening to us right now, too," Hal said. "His instruments are extremely sensitive. Still, the walls are heavily soundproofed. Anyway, forget about him!"

Fobo followed him into his rooms. The wog felt Jeannette's forehead and tried to lift her lid to look at her eye. It would not bend.

"Hmm! Calcification of the outer skin layer is far advanced."

With one hand he threw the sheet from her figure and with the other he grabbed her gown by the neckline and ripped the thin cloth down the middle. The two parts fell to either side. She lay nude, as silent and pale and beautiful as a sculptor's masterpiece.

Her lover gave a little cry at what seemed like a violation. But he said nothing because he realized that Fobo's move was medical. In any case, the wog would not have been sexually interested.

Puzzled, he watched. Fobo had tapped his fingertips against her flat belly and then put his ear against it. When he stood up, he shook his head.

"I won't deceive you, Hal. Though we'll do the best we can, we may not be good enough. She'll have to go to a surgeon. If we can cut her eggs out before they hatch, that, plus the serum you gave her, may reverse the effect and pull her out."

"Eggs?"

"I'll tell you later. Wrap her up. I'll run upstairs and phone Dr. Kuto."

Yarrow folded a blanket around her. Then he rolled her over. She was as stiff as a show-window dummy. He covered her face. The stony look was too much for him.

His wristphone shrilled. Automatically, he reached to flick the stud and just in time drew his hand back. It shrilled loudly, insistently. After a few seconds of agony, he decided that if he didn't answer, he would stir up their suspicion far faster.

"Yarrow!"

"Shib?"

"Report to the Archurielite. You will be given fifteen minutes."

"Shib."

Fobo came back in and said, "What're you going to do?"

Hal squared his mouth and said, "You take her by the shoulders, and I'll carry her feet. Rigid as she is, we won't need a stretcher."

As they carried her down the steps, he said, "Can you hide us after the operation, Fobo? We won't be able to use the gig now."

"Don't worry," the wog said enigmatically over his shoulder. "The Earthmen are going to be too busy to run after you."

It took sixty seconds to get her into the gig, hop to the hospital, and get her out.

Hal said, "Let's put her on the ground a minute. I've got to set the gig on auto and send her back to the *Gabriel*. That way, at least, they won't know where I am."

"No. Leave it here. You may be able to use it afterward."

"After what?"

"Later. Ah, there's Kuto."

In the waiting room, Hal paced back and forth and puffed Merciful Seraphim out in chains of smoke. Fobo sat on a chair and rubbed his bald pate and the thick golden corkscrew fuzz on the back of his head.

"All of this might have been avoided," he said unhappily. "If I had known the *lalitha* was living with you, I might have guessed why you wanted the Easyglow. Though not necessarily so. Anyway, I didn't find out until two days ago that she was in your apartment. And I was too busy with Project Earthman to think much about her."

"Project Earthman?" said Hal. "What's that?"

Fobo's V-in-V lips parted in a smile to reveal the sharp serrated ridges of bone.

"I can't tell you now because your colleagues on the *Gabriel* might, just possibly, learn about it from you before it takes effect. However, I think I can safely tell you that we know about your plan for spreading the deadly globin-locking molecule through our atmosphere."

"There was a time when I would have been horrified to learn that," Hal said. "But now it doesn't matter."

"You don't want to know how we found out about it?"

"I suppose so," Hal said dully.

"When you asked us for samples of blood, you aroused our suspicion."

He tapped the end of his absurdly long nose.

"We can't read your thoughts, of course. But concealed in this flesh are two antennae. They are very sensitive; evolution has not dulled our sense of smell as it has among you Terrans. They allow us to detect, through odor, very slight changes in the metabolism of others. When we were asked by one of your emissaries to donate blood for their scientific research, we smelled a—shall I call it *furtive?*—emanation. We finally did give you the blood. But it was that of a barnyard creature which uses copper in its blood cells. We wogs use magnesium as the oxygen-carrying element in our blood cells."

"Our virus is useless!"

"Yes. Of course, in time, when you'd learned to read our writing and got hold of our textbooks, you'd have discovered the truth. But before that happened it would be too late, I trust, hope, and pray, for the truth to be of any importance or consequence.

"Meanwhile, we've determined just what you were up to. I'm sorry to say that we had to use force to do it, but since our survival was at stake and you Earthmen were the aggressor, the means justified the ends. A week ago we finally found an opportunity to catch a biochemist and his *gapt* while they were visiting a laboratory in the college. We injected a drug and hypnotized them. It was difficult getting the truth out of them but only because of the language barrier. However, I've learned a certain amount of American.

"We were horrified. But not really surprised. In fact, because we suspected something was afoot that we wouldn't like, and from the very first contact, we were ready to take action. So, from the first day your ship landed, we've been busy. The vessel, as you know, is directly—"

"Why didn't you hypnotize me?" Hal said. "You could have done it easily and a long time ago."

"Because we doubted that you'd be privy to anything that had to do with our blood. Anyway, we needed someone who had the necessary technical knowledge. However, we've been watching you, though not so successfully, since you managed to sneak in the *lalitha* past us."

"How did you find out about Jeannette?" Hal said. "And may I see her?"

"I am sorry; I must say no to your second question," said Fobo. "As for the first, it was not until two days ago that we managed to develop a listening device sensitive enough to justify installing it in your rooms. As you know, we are far behind you in some departments."

"I searched the *puka* every day for a long time," said Hal. "Then, when I learned of the stage of development of your electronics, I quit."

"Meanwhile, our scientists have been busy," said Fobo. "The visit of you Earthmen has stimulated us to research in several fields."

A nurse entered and said, "Phone, Doctor."

Fobo left.

Yarrow paced back and forth and smoked another cigarette. Within a minute, Fobo returned.

He said, "We're going to have company. One of my colleagues, who is watching the ship, tells me Macneff and two Uzzites left in a gig. They should be arriving at the hospital any second now."

Yarrow stopped in midstride. His jaw dropped. "Here? How'd they find out?"

"I imagine they have means about which they failed to inform you. Don't be afraid."

Hal stood motionless. The cigarette, unnoticed, burned until it seared his fingers. He dropped it and crushed it beneath his sole.

Boot heels clicked in the corridor.

Three men entered. One was a tall and gaunt ghost —Macneff, the Archurielite. The others were short and broad-shouldered and clad in black. Their meaty hands, though empty, were hooked, ready to dart into their pockets. Their heavy-lidded eyes stabbed at Fobo and then at Hal.

Macneff strode up to the *joat*. His pale blue eyes

glared; his lipless mouth was drawn back in a skull's smile.

"You unspeakable degenerate!" he shouted.

His arm flashed, and the whip, jerked out of his belt, cracked. Thin red marks appeared on Yarrow's white face and began oozing blood.

"You will be taken back to Earth in chains and there exhibited as an example of the worst pervert, traitor, and—and—!"

He drooled, unable to find words.

"You—who have passed the Elohimeter, who are supposed to be so pure—you have lusted after and lain with an insect!"

"What!"

"Yes. With a thing that is even lower than a beast of the field! What even Moses did not think of when he forbade union between man and beast, what even the Forerunner could not have guessed when he re-affirmed the law and set the utmost penalty for it—you have done! You, Hal Yarrow, the pure, the *lamedh*-wearer!"

Fobo rose and said in a deep voice, "Might I suggest and stress that you are not quite right in your zoological classification? It is not the class of *Insecta* but the class of the *Chordata pseudarthropoda,* or words to that effect."

Hal said, "What?" He could not think.

The wog growled, "Shut up. Let me talk."

He swung to face Macneff. "You know about her?"

"You are *shib* that I know her! Yarrow thought he was getting away with something. But, no matter how clever these unrealists are, they're always tripped up. In this case, it was his asking Turnboy about those Frenchmen that fled Earth. Turnboy, who is very zealous in his attitude toward the Sturch, reported the conversation. It lay among my papers for quite a while. When I came across it, I turned it over to the psychologists. They told me that the *joat's* question was a deviation from the pattern expected of him; a thing totally irrelevant unless it was connected to something we didn't know about him.

"Moreover, his refusal to grow a beard was enough to make us suspicious. A man was put on his trail. He saw Yarrow buying twice the groceries he should have. Also, when you wogs learned the tobacco habit from us and began making cigarettes too, he bought them from you. The conclusion was obvious. He had a female in his apartment.

"We didn't think it'd be a wog. female, for she wouldn't have to stay hidden. Therefore, she must be human. But we couldn't imagine how she got here on Ozagen. It was impossible for him to have stowed her away on the *Gabriel*. She must either have come here in a different ship or be descended from people who had.

"It was Yarrow's talk with Turnboy that furnished the clue. Obviously, the French had landed here and she was a descendant. We didn't know how the *joat* had found her. It wasn't important. We'll find out, anyhow."

"You're due to find out some other things, too," Fobo said calmly. "How did you discover she wasn't human?"

Yarrow muttered, "I've got to sit down."

19

HE swayed to the wall and sank into a chair. One of the Uzzites started to move toward him. Macneff waved the man back and said, "Turnboy got a wog to read to him a book on the history of man on Ozagen. He came across so many references to the *lalitha* that the suspicion was bound to rise that the girl might be one.

"Last week one of the wog physicians, while talking to Turnboy, mentioned that he had once examined a *lalitha*. Later, he said, she had run away. It wasn't hard for us to guess where she was hiding!"

"My boy," said Fobo, turning to Hal, "didn't you read We'enai's book?"

Hal shook his head. "We started it, but Jeannette mislaid it."

"And doubtless saw to it that you had other things to think of . . . they are good at diverting a man's mind. Why not? That is their purpose in life.

"Hal, I'll explain. The *lalitha* are the highest example of mimetic parasitism known. Also, they are unique among sentient beings. Unique in that all are female.

"If you'd read on in We'enai, you'd have found that fossil evidence shows that about the time that Ozagenian man was still an insectivorous marmoset-like creature, he had in his family group not only his

185

own females but the females of another phylum. These animals looked and probably stank enough like the females of prehomo marmoset to be able to live and mate with them. They seemed mammalian, but dissection would have indicated their pseudoarthropodal ancestry.

"It's reasonable to suppose that these precursors of the *lalitha* were man's parasites long before the marmosetoid stage. They may have met him when he first crawled out of the sea. Originally bisexual, they became female. And they adapted their shape, through an unknown evolutionary process, to that of the reptile's and primitive mammal's. And so on.

"What we do know is that the *lalitha* was Nature's most amazing experiment in parasitism and parallel evolution. As man metamorphosed into higher forms, so the *lalitha* kept pace with him. All female, mind you, depending upon the male of another phylum for the continuance of the species.

"It is astonishing the way they became integrated into the prehuman societies, the pithecanthropoid and neanderthaloid steps. Only when *Homo sapiens* developed did their troubles begin. Some families and tribes accepted them; others killed them. So they resorted to artifice and disguised themselves as human women. A thing not hard to do—unless they became pregnant.

"In which case, they died."

Hal groaned and put his hands over his face.

"Painful but real, as our acquaintance Macneff would say," said Fobo. "Of course—such a condition required a secret sorority. In those societies where the *lalitha* was forced to camouflage, she would, once pregnant, have to leave. And perish in some hidden place among her kind, who would then take care of the nymphs"—here Hal shuddered—"until they were able to go into human cultures. Or else be introduced as foundlings or changelings.

"You'll find quite a tribal lore about them—fables and myths make them central or peripheral characters quite frequently. They were regarded as witches, demons, or worse.

"With the introduction of alcohol in primitive times, a change for the better came to the *lalitha.* Alcohol made them sterile. At the same time, barring accident, disease, or murder, it made them *immortal.*"

Hal took his hands off his face. "You—you mean Jeannette would have lived—forever? That I cost her —that?"

"She could have lived many thousands of years. We know that some did. What's more, they did not suffer physical deterioration but always remained at the physiological age of twenty-five. Let me explain all this. In due order. Some of what I'm going to tell you will distress you. But it must be said.

"The long lives of the *lalitha* resulted in their being worshipped as goddesses. Sometimes, they lived so long they survived the downfall of mighty nations that had been small tribes when the *lalitha* first joined their groups. The *lalitha,* of course, became the repositories of wisdom, wealth, and power. Religions were established in which the *lalitha* was the immortal goddess, and the ephemeral kings and priests were her lovers.

"Some cultures outlawed the *lalitha.* But these either directed the nations they ruled into conquering the people that rejected them or else infiltrated and eventually ruled as powers behind the throne. Being always very beautiful, they became the wives and mistresses of the most influential men. They competed with the human female and beat them at their own game, hands down. In the *lalitha,* Nature wrought the complete female.

"And so they gained mastery over their lovers. But not over themselves. Though they belonged to a secret society in the beginning, they soon enough split up. They began to identify themselves with the nations they ruled and to use their countries against the others. Moreover, their long lives resulted in younger *lalitha* becoming impatient. Result: assassinations, struggles for power, and so on.

"Also, their influence was technologically too stabilizing. They tried to keep the *status quo* in every aspect of culture, and as a result the human cultures had a tendency to eliminate all new and progressive ideas and the men that espoused them."

Fobo paused, then said, "You must realize that most of this is speculative. It's based largely on what the very few human natives we've captured in the jungle have told us. However, we recently discovered some pictographs in a long-buried temple that gave us additional information. So we think our reconstruction of the history of the *lalitha* is valid.

"Oh, by the way, Jeannette didn't have to run away from us. After we'd learned all we could from her, we'd have returned her to her family. We told her we would, but she didn't believe us."

A wog nurse came out of the operating room and said something to the empathist in a low voice.

Macneff walked by her and obviously tried to eavesdrop. But as the nurse was speaking in Ozagenian, which he did not understand, he continued pacing back and forth. Hal wondered why he, Hal, had not been dragged away at once, why the priest had waited to hear Fobo out. Then, a flash of insight told Hal that Macneff wanted him to hear all about Jeannette and realize the enormity of his deeds.

The nurse went back into the operating room. The Archurielite said loudly, "Is the beast of the fields dead yet?"

Hal shook as if he had been struck when he heard the word *dead*. But Fobo ignored the priest.

He spoke to Hal. "Your larv—that is, your children, have been removed. They are in an incubator. They are . . ." he hesitated—"eating well. They will live."

Hal knew from his tone that it was no use asking about the mother.

Big tears rolled from Fobo's round blue eyes.

"You won't understand what has happened, Hal, unless you comprehend the *lalitha's* unique method of reproduction. Three things the *lalitha* needs to reproduce. One thing must precede the other two. That primary event is to be infected at the age of puberty by another adult *lalitha*. This infection is needed to transmit genes."

"Genes?" said Hal. Even in his shock, he could feel interest and amazement at what Fobo was telling him.

"Yes. Since *lalitha* receive no genes from the human males, they must exchange hereditary material between each other. Yet—they must use man as a means.

"Allow and permit me to elucidate. An adult *lalitha* has three so-called banks of genes. Two are duplicates of each other's chromosomal stuff.

"The third, I will explain in a moment.

"A *lalitha's* uterus contains ova, the genes of which are duplicated in the bodies of microscopic wrigglers formed in the giant salivary glands in a *lalitha's* mouth. These wrigglers—salivary ova—are continually released by the adult.

"The adult *lalitha* pass genes by means of these invisible creatures; they infect each other as if the carriers of heredity were diseases. They cannot escape it; a kiss, a sneeze, a touch, will do it.

"Preadolescent *lalitha*, however, seem to have a natural immunity against being infected by these wrigglers.

"The adult *lalitha*, once infected, then builds up antibodies against reception of salivary ova from a second *lalitha*.

"Meanwhile, the first wrigglers she is exposed to have made their way through the bloodstream, the intestinal tract, the skin, boring, floating, until they arrive at the uterus of the host.

"There, the salivary ovum unites with the uterine ovum. Fusion of the two produces a zygote. At this point, fertilization is suspended. True, all genetic data needed to produce a new *lalitha* is provided. All except the genes for the specific features of the face of the baby. This data will be given by the male human lover of the *lalitha*. Not, however, until the conjunction of two more events.

"These two must occur simultaneously. One is excitation by orgasm. The other is stimulation of the photokinetic nerves. One cannot take place without the other. Neither can the last two come about unless the first happens. Apparently, fusion of the two ova causes a chemical change in the *lalitha* which then makes her capable of orgasm and fully develops the photokinetic nerves."

Fobo paused and cocked his head as if he were listening for something outside. Hal, who knew from familiarity with the wogs what their facial expressions meant, felt that Fobo was waiting for something important to happen. Very important. And, whatever it was, it involved the Earthmen.

Suddenly, he thrilled to the knowledge that he was on the wogs' side! He was no longer an Earthman, or, at least, not a Haijac.

"Are you sufficiently confused?" said Fobo.

"Sufficiently," replied Hal. "For instance, I have never heard of the photokinetic nerves."

"The photokinetic nerves are the exclusive property of the *lalitha*. They run from the retina of the eye, along with the optic nerves, to the brain. But the photokinetic nerves descend the spinal column and leave its base to enter the uterus. The uterus is not that of the human female. Do not even compare them. You might say that the *lalitha* uterus is the darkroom of the womb. Where the photograph of the father's face is biologically developed. And, in a manner of speaking, attached to the daughters' faces.

"This is done by means of photogenes. These are in the third bank of which I spoke. You see, during intercourse, at the moment of orgasm, an electrochemical change, or series of changes, takes place in that nerve. By the light that the *lalitha* requires during intercourse if she is to experience orgasm, the face of the male is photographed. An arc-reflex makes it impossible for her to close her eyes at that time. Moreover, if she throws her arm over her eyes, she at once loses the orgasm.

"You must have noticed during your intercourse with her, for I'm sure she insisted you keep your eyes open, that her pupils contracted to a pinpoint. That contraction was an involuntary reflex which would narrow her field of vision to your face. Why? So the photokinetic nerves could receive data from only your face. Thus, the information about the specific color of your hair could be passed on to the bank of photogenes. We don't know the exact manner in which the photokinetic nerves transmit this data. But they do it.

"Your hair is auburn. Somehow, this information becomes known to the bank. The bank then rejects the other genes controlling other colors of hair. The 'auburn' gene is duplicated and attached to the zygote's genetic makeup. And so with the other genes that fix the other features of the face-to-be. The shape of the nose—modified to be feminine—is selected by choosing the correct combination of genes in the bank. This is duplicated, and the duplicates are then incorporated into the zygote—"

"You hear that?" shouted Macneff in an exultant voice. "You have begat larvae! Monsters of an unholy unreal union! Insect children! And they will have your face as witness of this revolting carnality—"

"Of course, I am no connoisseur of human features," Fobo interrupted. "But the young man's strike me as vigorous and handsome. In a human way, you understand."

He turned to Hal. "Now you see why Jeannette desired light. And why she pretended alcoholism. As long as she had enough liquor before copulation, the photokinetic nerve—very susceptible to alcohol—would be anesthetized. Thus, orgasm but no pregnancy. No death from the life within her. But when you diluted the beetlejuice with Easyglow . . . unknowing, of course—"

Macneff burst into a high-pitched laughter. "What irony! Truly it has been said that the wages of unrealism are death!"

20

FOBO spoke loudly. "Go ahead, Hal. Cry, if you like. You'll feel better. You can't, eh? I wish you could.

"Very well, I continue. The *lalitha*, no matter how human she looks, cannot escape her arthropod heritage. The nymphs that develop from the larvae can easily pass for babies, but it would pain you to see the larvae themselves. Though they are not any uglier than a five months' human embryo. Not to me, anyway.

"It is a sad thing that the *lalitha* mother must die. Hundreds of millions of years ago, when a primitive pseudoarthropod was ready to hatch the eggs in her womb, a hormone was released in her body. It calcified the skin and turned her into a womb-tomb. She became a shell. Her larvae ate the organs and the bones, which were softened by the draining away of their calcium. When the young had fulfilled the function of the larva, which is to eat and grow, they rested and became nymphs. Then they broke the shell in its weak place in the belly.

"That weak point is the navel. It alone does not calcify with the epidermis but remains soft. By the time the nymphs are ready to come out, the soft flesh of the navel has decayed. Its dissolution lets loose a chemical which decalcifies an area that takes in most

193

of the abdomen. The nymphs, though weak as human babies and much smaller, are activated by instinct to kick out the thin and brittle covering.

"You must understand, Hal, that the navel itself is both functional and mimetic. Since the larvae are not connected to the mother by an umbilical cord, they would have no navel. But they grow an excrescence that resembles one.

"The breasts of the adult also have two functions. Like the human female's, they are both sexual and reproductive. They never produce milk, of course, but they are glands. At the time the larvae are ready to hatch from the eggs, the breasts act as two powerful pumps of the hormone which carries out the hardening of the skin.

"Nothing wasted, you see—Nature's economy. The things that enable her to survive in human society also carry out the death process."

"I can understand the need for photogenes in the humanoid stage of evolution," Hal said. "But when the *lalitha* were in the animal stage of evolution, why should they need to reproduce the characteristics of the father's face? There isn't much difference between the face of a male animal and a female animal of the same species."

"I do not know," said Fobo. "Perhaps, the prehuman *lalitha* did not utilize the photokinetic nerves. Perhaps, those nerves are an evolutionary adaptation of an existing structure which had a different function. Or a vestigial function. There is some evidence that photokinesis was the means by which the *lalitha* changed her body to conform with the change in the human body as it passed up the evolutionary ladder. It seems reasonable to suppose that the *lalitha* needed such a biological device. If the photokinetic nerves were not involved, some other organ may have been. It is unfortunate that by the time we were advanced enough to scientifically study the *lalitha,* we had no specimens available. Finding Jeannette was pure luck. We did discover in her several organs whose functions remain a mystery to us. We need many of her kind for fruitful research."

"One more question," said Hal. "What if a *lalitha* had more than one lover? Whose features would her baby have?"

"If a *lalitha* were raped by a gang, she would not have an orgasm because the negative emotions of fear and disgust would bar it. If she had more than one lover—and she weren't drinking alcohol—she would reproduce young whose features would be those of the first lover. By the time she lay with her second lover—even if it were immediately afterward—the complete fertilization would have already been initiated."

Sorrowfully, Fobo shook his head.

"It is a sad thing, but it has not changed in all these epochs. The mothers must give their lives for their young. Yet Nature, as a sort of recompense, has given them a gift. On the analogy of reptiles, which, it is said, do not stop growing larger as long as they are alive, the *lalitha* will not die if they remain unpregnant. And so—"

Hal leaped to his feet and shouted, "Stop it!"

"I'm sorry," Fobo said softly. "I'm just trying to make you see why Jeannette felt that she couldn't tell you what she truly was. She must have loved you, Hal. She possessed the three factors that make love: a genuine passion, a deep affection, and the feeling of being one flesh with you, male and female so inseparable it would be hard to tell where one began and the other ended. I know she did, believe me, for we empathists can put ourselves into somebody else's nervous system and think and feel as they do.

"Yet, Jeannette must have had a bitter leaven in her love. The belief that if you knew she was of an utterly alien branch of the animal kingdom, separated by millions of years of evolution, barred by her ancestry and anatomy from the true completion of marriage—children—you would turn from her with horror. That belief must have shot with darkness even her brightest moments—"

"*No!* I would have loved her anyway! It might have been a shock. But I'd have gotten over it. Why, she was human; she was more human than any woman I've known!"

Macneff sounded as if he were going to retch. When he had recovered himself, he howled, "You abysmal thing! How can you stand yourself now that you know what utterly filthy monster you have lain with! Why don't you try to tear out your eyes, which have seen that vile filth! Why don't you bite off your lips, which have kissed that insect mouth! Why don't you cut off your hands, which have pawed with loathsome lust that mockery of a body! Why don't you tear out by the roots those organs of carnal—"

Fobo spoke through the storm of wrath. "Macneff! Macneff!"

The gaunt head swiveled toward the empathist. His eyes stared, and his lips had drawn back into what seemed to be an impossibly large smile; a smile of absolute fury.

"What? What?" he muttered, like a man waking from sleep.

"Macneff, I know your type well. Are you sure you weren't planning on taking the *lalitha* alive and using her for your own sensual purposes? Doesn't most of your fury and disgust result from being balked in your desires? After all, you've not had a woman for a year, and . . ."

The Sandalphon's jaw fell. Red flooded his face and became purple. The violent color faded, and a corpse-like white replaced it.

He screeched like an owl.

"*Enough!* Uzzites, take this—this thing that calls itself a man to the gig!"

The two men in black circled to come at the *joat* from front and back. Their approach was based on training, not caution. Years of taking prisoners had taught them to expect no resistance. The arrested always stood cowed and numb before the representatives of the Sturch. Now, despite the unusual circumstances and the knowledge that Hal carried a gun, they saw nothing different in him.

He stood with bowed head and hunched shoulders and dangling arms, the typical arrestee.

That was one second; the next, he was a tiger striking.

The agent in front of him reeled back, blood flowing from his mouth and spilling on his black jacket. When he bumped into the wall, he paused to spit out teeth.

By then, Yarrow had whirled and rammed a fist into the big soft belly of the man behind him.

"Whoof!" went the Uzzite.

He folded. As he did so, Hal brought his knee up against the unguarded chin. There was a crack of bone breaking, and the agent fell to the floor.

"Watch him!" Macneff yelled. "He's got a gun!"

The Uzzite by the wall shoved his hand under his jacket, feeling for the weapon in his armpit holster. Simultaneously, a heavy bronze bookend, thrown by Fobo, struck his temple. He crumpled.

Macneff screamed, "You are resisting, Yarrow! You are resisting!"

Hal bellowed, "You're damn *shib* I am!"

Head down, he plunged at the Sandalphon.

Macneff slashed with his whip at his attacker. The seven lashes wrapped themselves around Hal's face, but he rammed into the purple-clad form and knocked it down on the floor.

Macneff got to his knees; Hal, also on his knees, seized Macneff by the throat and squeezed.

Macneff's face turned blue, and he grabbed Hal's wrists and tried to tear them away. But Hal squeezed harder.

"You . . . can't do . . . this!" said Macneff, wheezing. "Can't . . . impossi—"

"I can! I can!" screamed Hal. "I've always wanted to do this, Pornsen! I mean . . . Macneff!"

At that moment, the floors shook, the windows rattled. Almost immediately, a tremendous *boom*! blew in the windows. Glass flew; Hal was hurled to the floor.

Outside, the night became day. Then, night again.

Hal rose to his feet. Macneff lay on the floor, his hands feeling his neck.

"What was that?" Hal said to Fobo.

Fobo went to the broken window and looked out. He was bleeding from a cut on his neck, but he did not seem to notice it.

"It's what I've been waiting for," Fobo said.

He turned to face Hal.

"From the moment the *Gabriel* landed, we've been digging under it, and—"

"Our sound-detection equipment—"

"—caught the noise of the underground trains directly below the ship. But we dug only when the trains were moving through so the digging would be covered up. Normally, a train would go through the tunnels every ten minutes. But we routed them through every two minutes or so and made sure that they were long freight trains.

"Only a few days ago we completed filling the hole under the *Gabriel* with gunpowder. Believe me, we all breathed easier after it was done, for we'd feared we might be heard despite our precautions or that our shorings might break under the great weight of the ship. Or that, for some reason, the captain might decide to move the ship."

"Then you blew it up?" Hal said dazedly.

Things were going too fast for him.

"I doubt that. Even with the tons of explosives we set off, they could not damage too much a vessel built as solidly as the *Gabriel*. As a matter of fact, we did not wish to damage it, for we want to study it.

"But our calculations showed that the shock waves going through the metal plates of the ship would kill every man in the ship."

Hal went to the window and looked out. Against the moon-bright sky was a pillar of smoke; soon, the entire city would be covered with it.

"You had better get your men aboard at once," Hal said. "If the explosion only knocked out the officers on the bridge, and they regain consciousness before you reach them, they will press a button that will trigger an H-bomb.

"This will blow everything up for miles around. Its explosion will make your powder charge seem a baby's breath. Far worse, it will release a deadly radioactivity that will kill millions more—if the winds go inland."

Fobo turned pale, though he tried to smile.

"I imagine our soldiers are on board by now. But I'll phone them just to make sure."

He returned after a minute. Now, he did not have to make an effort to smile.

"Everyone on board the *Gabriel* died instantly, including the personnel on the bridge. I've told the captain of the boarding party not to tamper with any mechanisms or controls."

"You've thought of everything, haven't you?" Hal said.

Fobo shrugged, and he said, "We are fairly peaceful. But, unlike you Terrans, we are really 'realists.' If we have to take action against vermin, we do our best to exterminate them. On this insect-ridden planet we have had a long history of battling killers."

He looked at Macneff, who was on all fours, eyes glazed, shaking his head like a wounded bear.

Fobo said, "I do not include you in the vermin, Hal. You are free to go where you want, do what you want."

Hal sat down in a chair. He said, in a grief-husked voice, "I think that all my life I've wanted just that. Freedom to go where I wanted, do what I wanted. But, now, what is there left for me? I have no one—"

"There is much for you, Hal," said Fobo. Tears ran down his nose and collected at the end.

"You have your daughters to care for, to love. In a short time, they will be through with their feeding in the incubator—they survived the premature removal quite well—and will be beautiful babies. They will be yours as much as any human infants could be.

"After all, they look like you—in a modified feminine way, of course. Your genes are theirs. What's the difference whether genes act by cellular or photonic means?

"Nor will you be without women. You forget that she has aunts and sisters. All young and beautiful. I'm sure that we can locate them."

Hal buried his face in his hands, and he said, "Thanks, Fobo, but that's not for me."

"Not now," Fobo said softly. "But your grief will soften; you will think life worth living again."

Someone came into the room. Hal looked up to see a nurse.

"Doctor Fobo, we are bringing the body out. Does the man care for one last look?"

Hal shook his head. Fobo walked over to him and put his hand on his shoulder.

"You look faint," he said. "Nurse, do you have some smelling salts?"

Hal said, "No, I won't need them."

Two nurses wheeled a carrier out. A white sheet was draped over the shell. Black hair cascaded from beneath the sheet and fell over the pillow.

Hal did not rise. He sat in the chair, and he moaned, "Jeannette! Jeannette! If you had only loved me enough to tell me . . . "

Exciting Space Adventure from DEL REY